'What do you want, Stev?

Those enticing blue [...] oned. 'I want persua[...]

Catherine gave him a [...] the most insulting thing[...] to me. Whatever you [...] never cheapened myself to [...] nan sexual favours to gain what I want. And I don't intend to start now!'

Steve laughed, unmoved by her protestations. 'I'm afraid you're in the grown-up league now, sweetheart!'

Dear Reader

Falling in love is exciting. . .but we all know that it *can* be complicated! For instance, what would you do if the man of your dreams happened to be your father's worst enemy? That's the dilemma faced by Charlotte Lamb's heroine next month in **DEADLY RIVALS**, the second book in her compelling new series—don't miss it! And you'll find some thrilling love-stories in *this* month's selection, too. All our authors love to create really special romances—we hope you enjoy this one!

The Editor

Christine Greig works full-time as a senior marketing manager in the communications industry. This involves a great deal of travel, both within Europe and the United States, which she enjoys very much. She has a BA Hons degree and a diploma in marketing. She is in her thirties, came originally from North Yorkshire, England, and is married.

Recent titles by the same author:

PASSIONATE OBSESSION

WICKED SEDUCTION

BY

CHRISTINE GREIG

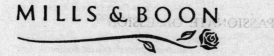

MILLS & BOON

*MILLS & BOON and the Rose Device
are trademarks of the publisher.
Harlequin Mills & Boon Limited,
Eton House, 18-24 Paradise Road, Richmond, Surrey, TW9 1SR
This edition published by arrangement with Harlequin Enterprises B.V.*

© Christine Greig 1995

ISBN 0 263 78985 3

*Set in Linotron Times 10 on 11.25 pt
01-9505-53814*

*Typeset in Great Britain by Centracet, Cambridge
Made and printed in Great Britain*

CHAPTER ONE

CAT FARRELL shook her hair out of her riding hat, letting the jet-black waves cascade silkily around her shoulders. Her sheer jubilance was infectious, her dark eyes alight with pleasure. Laughing, her white teeth revealed in their pearly perfection, she acknowledged the crowd.

'. . .first prize in the senior section, with also the junior championship behind her, clearly set for a magnificent career—Catherine Farrell.'

Patting her horse, Shannon, Cat headed for the paddock at a gentle trot. What a day! Her name on the ancient silver of the Chalfont Cup. It was a dream come true! Today was a golden day. A day when the pressing complexities of life could be forgotten. But it wasn't that easy! Chas Lucas applauded her from the members' stand and the problems caused by the purchase of Ranleigh Manor flooded back.

Ranleigh had been home for the Farrells for over a century and now that Edward, the last of the Ranleigh line, was dead, the manor house had been sold to Lucas-Brett. It had been a shrewd manoeuvre by the international property developers. The Ranleigh estate was flanked ten miles to the east by Reading and to the west, almost the same distance away, by Swindon. The nearest village of any size was Barons Green, perched on the edge of Lambourn Downs. Pretty countryside within easy reach of the M4 was prime terrtory for development, and the area was peppered with wealthy entrepreneurs from London. Lucas-Brett intended to develop the estate into a hotel and golf course, and where exactly the Farrell stables fitted into that had yet to be decided. One thing was for sure: Ranleigh would not have to look far for customers wanting their leisure gilt-edged.

Conscious that Chas was following her to the paddock, she was surprised when a dark cloud momentarily blotted out the sun. Squinting against the sudden change of light, Cat was bemused as the bridle of her horse was caught and held and Chas Lucas smiled up at her. It wasn't Chas, however, who commanded her attention. Blue eyes reminiscent of hot desert skies blazed into hers. For a moment she forgot about Ranleigh, the Chalfont Cup. . . She was scorched by the sort of heat that bleached bones. Blinking, she realised that the tall stranger with the compelling gaze was restraining her horse's skittishness as a rumble of thunder growled in from the west.

'Felicity Barnhurst is holding a celebration party at Cranwell's. Are you coming, Cat?' Chas reclaimed her attention.

'I have to see to Shannon,' she began doubtfully, agilely slipping from the horse's back. 'I don't——'

Felicity appeared. 'Don't be silly, Cat. George will see to Shannon. Besides, that old bucket you transport this donkey in has a flat. So you can't make a quick getaway.'

Cat's heart sank. Felicity seized her arm, promising everything would be sorted out and that she needed a chance to enjoy herself.

Felicity Barnhurst was a childhood friend. A vibrant redhead, she shared Cat's obsession with horses.

'If George needs a break, let me know.' The dry American voice came from Chas's friend.

'Oh, this is Steve.' Chas slapped the man's shoulder.

'He's marvellous with anything mechanical. A regular grease monkey.'

Steve's blue eyes glittered with amusement, meeting Cat's with something in their depths that suggested he disapproved of her. Cat's shoulders stiffened and she tilted her nose in the air in true British toffee-nosed fashion.

'Bit of a dish.' Felicity was immune to the undercurrents. 'Who is he?'

'I've no idea.' Cat quickened her pace to leave the two men behind, tutting impatiently at her friend's lingering backward glance.

'I hope he comes to Cranwell's. Hurry up and get changed, Cat. I don't want Penelope Cheetham to nab him.'

Cat shook her head, amusement curling her mouth. She liked Felicity but they couldn't be more different. Talent kept her place with the 'horsey set'. She hadn't the position of privilege or money to mix with them on any other terms.

Cat was toasted loud and long at the old coaching inn chosen for the celebrations. Both Felicity and Penelope Cheetham were happy that the other hadn't won. Neither minded Cat's supremacy because, despite her raven-haired beauty, she didn't compete with them in any other sphere.

The silver cup was brought full to the brim of some innocuous-tasting punch. Across it, she caught sight of the blue-eyed stranger. He was older than most of her friends celebrating at Cranwell's. Early- to mid-thirties, she guessed, with a vast wealth of experience to back up that sleek air of sophistication. He was worth admiring and didn't he know it! Those remarkable eyes were fringed with long dark lashes, darkening his gaze so that it was like seeing the glitter of water through a weave of trees. Dark brown hair and eyebrows, a strong nose and firm sensuous lips added up to a potent image of masculinity.

'I wouldn't drink that if I were you.' His voice, smooth and warm as honey, insinuated itself despite the row.

Tension curled along her spine, her delicate nostrils quivering as the smoke and cacophony of sound played on her senses. She had been sensible, responsible and of unimpeachable virtue for most of her young life and she had never felt more in need of a day off. Steve, whatever his name was, seemed determined to act as her conscience.

With slow deliberation, she lifted the cup and drank deeply, her eyes fixed on the 'been everywhere and done everything' Yank.

'It's your funeral.' He made her feel like an excitable adolescent. That lurking criticism was there again, lighting embers of recklessness she hadn't known she possessed.

'Lighten up, Steve.' Chas pushed a glass of whisky at him. 'Cat's just fulfilled a lifetime ambition. She can afford to let her hair down.'

'It's beautiful hair.' Steve appeared to take his friend's advice, raising the glass to his lips and savouring a mouthful.

The self-conscious flush that stained Cat's cheeks was met with cynical disbelief.

'You're young to fulfil lifetime ambitions. You've either packed a lot into your tender years or you have limited horizons.'

Cat almost gasped at his sheer, unadulterated rudeness.

'I'm old enough to have learnt some manners, Mr. . .?' His raised eyebrow derided her as if he considered her unworthy of battle. What the battle was she didn't know but this man didn't believe in warning shots, he stormed the barricades.

'Blame it on jet-lag,' Chas intervened with haste. 'Steve, let me introduce you to the Cheethams. The Colonel's very influential in the county.'

'I wouldn't like to spoil a golden moment.' Steve was perfectly aware of Chas's diversionary tactics. The low, mocking, 'I'll be back,' was for Cat's ears only.

Following her adversary's progress towards the waiting Cheethams, Cat was besieged by doubts about the future. The Farrell connection with Ranleigh was one born out of the peculiarities of patronage. The stables belonged to the Farrells but her family home, Primrose Cottage, was part of the estate. Jessica Farrell, her beloved and usually mild-mannered parent, had dug in her heels and stubbornly refused to consider moving. Any major disturbance in her life brought on severe asthmatic attacks and Cat's concern over her mother's health had made her set clear terms for any sale. She was determined that any negotiations would include the cottage and, if possible, the re-siting of the stables.

Short acquaintance with Chas Lucas had led her to believe that a deal satisfactory to all sides could be negotiated. He was by no means a pushover but he had been sympathetic to her family's situation. The mysterious Steve was definitely more what she had been expecting from Lucas-Brett! He looked like a corporate gladiator.

Deciding that she needed to find out more about him, she gravitated subtly towards Steve, using acquaintances as cover to glean pickings from his conversation. Chas seemed to be welded to his side, impossible to isolate and interrogate on just how dangerous this stranger was to the Farrells' plans.

'Are you enjoying yourself?' Cat nearly jumped out of her skin, discovering Chas disappearing into the distance and that she had been cut out of the herd without even realising it.

'Yes.' Her startled eyes collided with Steve's as he absorbed every vestige of emotion evident on her small, delicately boned face. 'Are you?'

She tried to ignore the excesses of some of her friends, meeting his eyes, aware they had been recorded with cool, critical precision.

'Immensely.' His smile had the same critical quality. 'I like watching the idle rich at play.'

Viewing his casual but expensive clothes, she gave him an enquiring look. 'You don't include yourself in that category, Mr. . .?'

'I work for a living, Miss Farrell. Can I call you Catherine? Cat sounds rather childish. You can call me Steve.'

'My friends call me Cat,' she replied guilelessly. 'By all means call me Catherine.'

Laughing softly, he viewed the tangled waves and curls surrounding her face appreciatively. Jet-black eyebrows above almond-shaped eyes lifted in faint reproof, emboldened by the unknown cocktail she had consumed.

'I'm told you're more talented than your horse. The generally accepted opinion is that you'd be a contender with the right money behind you.'

Her mouth tightened. That didn't sound like a compliment! She regarded him with suspicion. Recalling her mission, she decided to ignore the provocative overtones.

'Shannon might not be the best horse in the world but he puts his whole heart into it. That's worth a lot. I think so, anyway.'

'Bravo.' He toasted her, making her feel she had just won a prize at Speech Day. He winced as someone jostled his arm.

'Hey, stop ogling my girl.' Chas grinned, a distinct warning in his eyes when he met Cat's startled expression. 'Is no woman safe?'

'Catherine's as safe as she wants to be.' Steve flicked a glance at the glass the younger man offered her.

On the point of refusing, Cat was perplexed by feelings of rebellion. This man was imposing his judgement and she didn't like that. She would rather have fruit juice, but he made her feel as if she was seeking his approbation if she refused the drink. His searching glance fixed on her brother Jamie, who was impressing a bunch of his cronies by juggling with three oranges and causing havoc in the process. The drink represented allegiance and she drank it, her lashes sweeping upwards to meet the steady regard that mocked her mercilessly.

The party went on until evening. Steve asked her to dance and, mindful of her fact-finding mission, Cat agreed.

'Are you staying long in England?' she asked, hiding her discomfort at being taken in his arms, despite the similar dancing style adopted by those around them.

Blue eyes tangled with hers devilishly. 'A matter of hours rather than days.'

Her relief was almost tangible on the air. She relaxed against him for a moment, his aftershave teasing her nostrils. She breathed in his scent, the warmth of his body singeing her skin and making her eyes almost black with the shock of it.

'Why do I get the feeling you're glad about that?' His comment was teasing as if he was aware of her

distrust and found it amusing. It certainly wasn't a
question that demanded an answer.

'You're dangerous.' Had she really said that? Cat
nearly died with embarrassment. Why did she let fly
with the first thing that came into her head?

'I'm a pussy cat,' he growled back at her, genuinely
amused and for the first time lighting an answering
spark of humour in Cat. Her chuckle was a husky
attractive sound. His arms tightened fractionally and
she was enveloped in his warmth once more.

'Chas tells me you're a tough businesswoman giving
him a hard time.' He detained her when the last strains
of the song faded away, lightly holding her, waiting for
the next dance to begin. 'Do you drive a hard bargain,
Catherine?'

She was aware of interested parties around them but
felt held there by invisible bonds.

'No. . .not usually. I mean, I run a stables. Lucas-
Brett want my land. . .' She wasn't telling him anything
he probably didn't know if he was Chas's friend, but
suddenly that element of danger made the small hairs
at the back of her neck prickle warningly.

Drawing her closer, he rubbed the small of her back
comfortingly. 'You're a little thing to be up against a
multinational company. Doesn't it scare you, honey?'

His lean sinuous body nudged softly against hers as
he guided her through the other couples.

'Scare me?' She was breathless, as his fingers massaged her spine, causing a golden cascade of sparks to
electrify her bloodstream. 'No!' The protest was more
against being seduced on the dance floor than a denial
of the might of Lucas-Brett.

'No, I guess not.' Lips feathered her cheek, his
breath hot against her neck as they whispered softly in
her ear. 'Having the stables smack on the sixteenth

green of the golf course is something of a trump card. Do you know how to play it?'

The swift upward flick of her lashes met eyes of pure azure, a sexy smile mounting a devastating attack on every nerve in her body. 'Power is an aphrodisiac, so they say.' A flush spread over Catherine's throat at the intimacy of his gaze. It drew her in, sucked her into the heart of blue flame. 'It must give you quite a kick holding up a multimillion-dollar project.'

'No. . .' The denial was almost a whisper. Lucas-Brett had her equally at a disadvantage. They owned the land she used for pasture and access. It was pure distortion to imagine she had the international concern dangling on a string.

Steve was aware of several of the young men circling the dance-floor eyeing him with hostility. Chas had retreated, which didn't surprise him, and he needed more.

'You look tired.' He offered her the promise of escape.

'Yes.' Cat seized on the idea. 'I've been up since dawn. . .'

'I'll run you home.' The trap closed around her, smooth and steel-like. His fingers curved around her shoulder and he guided her from the dance-floor, his powerful, commanding figure melting a path through the crowd.

Cat was in his car, a sleek silver Mercedes, feeling her youthful reserves of independence and resourcefulness totally swamped by the man taking the wheel. His long fingers controlled the car with silken mastery, the Mercedes purring along the country roads, his profile set in concentration. Comparing him to Chas was like matching the leader of the pack with a puppy: no contest!

He found his way to Ranleigh with a minimum of directions. If it hadn't been for his assurance that he was merely passing through, Cat would have been seriously worried.

The sun was setting when they pulled up outside the cottage. Cat was pleased to see that the horse-box had returned. She hadn't liked leaving Shannon to strangers, even though she knew George was trust-worthy. The horse was her responsibility.

'Thank you for bringing me home.' She felt as if she was reciting lines from childhood, thanking someone's parent for allowing her to attend a party.

'I had an ulterior motive,' he owned up, watching her hand search the panel of the door to release it. 'There's no one at home.' His gaze briefly flickered over the darkened cottage. 'Is that usual?'

The warm confinement of the car created an intimacy that Cat found disturbing. Something new and danger-ous fluttered within her. She'd stopped her hunt for the door-handle and found herself drawn to the predatory waiting of his gaze.

'My mother will be back soon.' Her throat felt strangely constricted. She was entombed with him in a case of silver steel, panicked and intrigued at the same time.

'Don't you want to know what it is?' he queried, his voice deepening, making Cat's pulse riot.

'What?' She had lost the thread of the conversation, her eyes dark pools, reflecting the light of his penetrat-ing gaze.

'My motive.'

A breathless waiting drew the air tight around them, alive with tension, making Cat's mind giddy with the possibilities this man could offer her.

Long fingers cupped her cheek. His voice sounded

driven. 'What is Chas doing, leaving you alone with me? He must be mad.'

Dark lashes swept upwards. Her skin was very white, the excitement of the day and the lateness of the hour exaggerating the midnight darkness of her hair. 'Chas?'

'He's your boyfriend, isn't he?' He studied her closely.

'No, nothing like that. It's business really, but we've become friends——'

'Oh.' He nodded but didn't look convinced. 'Well, you need all the friends you can get.'

Something about the soft drawl and the slight curl of his lip troubled her. There was an indefinable menace about him and it frightened her. He let his thumb brush her cheek as if drawn to test its texture, the heel of his palm heating her jaw. His head dipped, his beautifully cut mouth moving to cover the quiver of her lips. It was the briefest of touches, designed to question her willingness, the leaving slightly more reluctant than the motive behind it dictated.

'Get going before I indulge my curiosity.'

'What?' The caress and husky tone of his voice lulled her senses. She nuzzled against his hand, disappointed when its heat faded and her cheek felt suddenly cold.

'I'd like to know whether you taste as delicious as you look.'

The words sent a stampede of excitement shimmering down her spine. With sudden decision, Steve got out of the car and came around to let her out. It was a gesture of old-fashioned courtesy underscored by purpose. Steve didn't intend the evening should get any more out of hand than it already had.

Cat floated to bed. Her mother was out visiting friends and Jamie had still to return from the party.

Her last thought before she slept was that she knew no more about who Steve was than she had done at the beginning.

The next morning, she woke up with a thumping headache with the prospect of mucking out the stables before her. The romantic glow of the evening before totally vanquished, she was left with the embarrassed knowledge that she had made an utter fool of herself and was lucky that the mysterious Steve had enough decency not to take advantage of her weakened state. Gratitude, however, did not noticeably colour her memories of the evening before. Steve had been up to something, and a brief holiday romance wasn't it!

Pulling on her clothes, she emerged into the daylight, her eyes narrowing as sunshine knifed into them, making her wince.

Cat was struck by a sudden wave of nostalgia, the familiar scene unfolding around her as she followed the path to the stables. Ranleigh Manor shimmered in the distance, a large, sprawling house with three gables, the grey flint-covered edifice softened by ivy. Cottages dotted the perimeter road, each with individual character, all neatly kept with a riot of colour in the garden. It was hard to imagine the Farrells exiled from Ranleigh. Cat was determined it wouldn't happen.

Shannon greeted her with a pleased snort when she approached his stable door. He didn't seem to have suffered from George's ministrations and she busied herself with mucking out the soiled straw while Trevor, the stable lad, led Shannon out to pasture.

Dressed in wellingtons, jeans and a white T-shirt, she took out her frustrations on wheeling the reeking wheat straw to the muck heap and then hosing down the floor and leaving it to dry. If Trevor and Johnnie, the two stable lads, found her sudden monopoly of this irksome job surprising they kept it to themselves, making her a strong cup of tea when she decided to take a break.

'Head lad at Lucas-Brett is up at Ranleigh,' Johnnie told her, meeting her swift attention with curiosity. 'The word is that he's not pleased with the way things are going and he's here to speed things up.'

Cat's spirits plummeted. 'Do you know what he's called?' she asked faintly.

'He's called Steve Lucas.' A familiar but dreaded voice came from behind her. 'Good morning, Catherine. Nice to see you up bright and early.'

Cat felt her face beat with heat. The stable lads were clearly surprised she was on first-name terms with the scourge of Lucas-Brett.

Steve Lucas was dressed in an expensive light grey suit, with a gleamingly white shirt and subdued tie. His dark hair was immaculately groomed and he presented a cultivated image amongst the tack-room's display of equine equipment.

'Cup of tea, Mr Lucas?' Trevor made up for Cat's lack of social niceties.

Steve nodded and sat down on one of the time-scarred wooden chairs. Cat stiffened as his long legs stretched out at an angle, blocking her way to the door. She didn't want him there! This was her retreat. She was the boss here, not Mr High-and-mighty Lucas.

'I thought Chas might have filled you in on a few background details.'

Cat Farrell gave him a long look, trying to judge the undercurrents in the conversation.

'He led me to believe he was in charge of the negotiations regarding Ranleigh.'

Steve Lucas let his gaze wander over her face,

speaking evenly despite the momentary pause as he watched her nervously moisten her lips.

'He's on site. Minor in-house problems I leave to junior management.'

'Is that what Farrells represents?' She was as matter-of-fact as he.

'It did. Thank you.' He accepted the tea and Trevor and Johnnie melted away, mumbling something about the horses.

'What can we have done to warrant your attention, Mr Lucas?' Cat's sarcasm had the effect of making her sound very young.

Steve Lucas raised the mug of tea to his lips and drank without wincing, which surprised Cat. Trevor's tea was something not-quite-of-this-world and was an acquired taste.

'Why did you lie to me about Chas? If you didn't know who I was, you risked messing things up flirting with me.'

'Messing things up?' Cat echoed, totally in the dark. 'I haven't the faintest——'

'Listen, sweetheart. Let's put the record straight. I've dealt with some high-class gold-diggers in my time and I can spot little amateurs like you with my eyes closed.' He watched the indignation surge through her with a hard uncompromising stare. 'I want the sale of Farrells to go through clean and businesslike with no unnecessary complications. Chas can wine and dine you on his own money and his own time. If this deal isn't settled soon, I'm taking over. Keep that in mind. I'm flying back to the States in a couple of hours. You have fair warning, when I meet up with you again, I won't play by the Queensberry rules.'

The conversation, she realised, had progressed along decidedly cryptic lines. He appeared to be under the mistaken impression that Chas had formed a romantic attachment to her and that she was using him to extend her bargaining power.

'I can asssure you that Chas hasn't in any way abused his expense account on my behalf. And as for flirting with you. . .all I'm guilty of was having too much to drink.'

'The cocktail was spiked. I did try to warn you.' Steve Lucas regarded her critically.

'It was a celebration,' she snapped. 'What were you on, bitter lemon?'

'I don't need to be on anything.'

'Lucky you.'

'So it seemed.'

The haunting memory of his mouth slowly brushing hers made Cat feel distinctly uncomfortable. The cocktail in the Chalfont Cup might well have been spiked but she hadn't been drunk. The alcohol had mellowed her usual reticence when it came to members of the opposite sex. The men she competed with in the show-ring had a way of trying to extend the competition to the bedroom. Having overheard their less than discreet bragging, she had no wish to favour any of them with a new conquest.

'So we've established I have a poor head for alcohol.' Cat's over-bright eyes showed her temper was on a hair trigger. 'What exactly were you doing last night, Mr Lucas? You knew who I was, so if anyone was being deceitful, it has to be you!'

'I was merely sizing up the opposition. A common business practice.' His eyes slid over her from her gypsy curls to her stained wellingtons. 'In your case, it was quite an enjoyable experience.'

Recognising the desirous look in his eyes, Cat jumped up, shaking her head in negation. 'Oh, no!

Believe me, I've learnt my lesson. I'm joining the temperance league, so the danger of such a nightmare recurring is extremely unlikely.'

'You think so?' He rose to his feet. The question was a blatant challenge and she was suddenly all too conscious of being backed up against the tack-room wall with nowhere to go.

'I'm positive.' A prickle of nervousness danced along her spine. 'What's the matter? Isn't the room big enough for you?'

'Sharp as a knife, aren't you?'

He might have left her then but she couldn't resist pushing her luck.

'I don't suppose you've ever seen *A Midsummer Night's Dream*?' Cat had a low opinion of the cultural advancement of her American cousins. She was allowed a moment's delight imagining him looking it up when he was miles away and discovering the insult. Comparing her enchantment the night before with the fairy queen's bewitched infatuation with a donkey would be suitable revenge for his scathing comments.

'Casting yourself in the role of Titania?' Male vanity alone would have demanded recompense. Cat had a second to realise that he wasn't the sort of man to mess with before he caught her elbows and jerked her towards him. A flash of blue seared her features before his mouth came down purposefully on hers.

It was then she discovered that temperance wasn't the answer. It hit her like an axe blow. His mouth was a hot, devouring predator. In a matter of seconds she was out of her depth and floundering in a bewildering whirlpool of sensation. He hauled her up against him, unbalancing her so that she was lying against his chest, her weight pulling his jacket apart, his body heat through the fine white linen a surge of flame against her skin.

Stunned, Cat felt her lips possessed and tutored in the art of pleasing. When her hand slipped inside his shirt in an effort to stop herself being crushed against his chest, the rasp of body hair against her fingers seemed to rob her lungs of air.

The shock was mutual. Steve kissed her as if he wanted to dismiss the night's magic in the cooler light of day. She aggravated him, daring to use her immature little-girl tricks on him. The last thing he needed was to get caught up in the same web as his fickle cousin. He wanted to stay angry and dismiss her with the contempt she deserved. Instead he found himself enjoying the rebellious sweetness of her mouth and the slight weight of her body panting against his harder frame. He resented Chas and his flimsy claim to being in love. He wanted this sham of innocence and passion with a fierceness that roared through his blood.

Cat's slender body bent, fight gone, like a reed in the wind, arching against him, aching for unknown pleasure. His marauding mouth moved over her small jawbone, seeking the delicate skin of her throat. Cat's lashes flickered as some sane part of herself surfaced slowly. She tensed, shocked as his hands moulded her hips and cupped her buttocks through the tightly stretched denim. It brought her into intimate contact with the hardening strength of his body. When the caress continued up to the waistband of her jeans and under her T-shirt, she recoiled from his touch.

'No!' The shock of hearing her own voice brought her to her senses. 'Get off me!' she shrieked, striking out wildly, her nails catching his neck and making him flinch backwards.

'Why you little. . .' He broke off, noticing the pallor

of her skin. She looked scared stiff and it stopped him dead in his tracks. A frown drew his brows together. 'What is it? This hot and cold routine of yours is a dangerous game, sweetheart.'

Her fingers forked through her fringe in a flustered gesture. 'I don't know how that happened.' She looked convincingly ashamed. 'It's. . .it's when you kiss me.' She moved back in case he should try again, staring at him wide-eyed, as if he was a time bomb and likely to go off. 'I've. . . I've never quite felt like that before.'

He studied her for what seemed an age and then his mouth twisted into a reluctant smile, a glimmer of amusement in the intensity of his gaze. 'What a flattering brush-off.'

'I'm sorry.' She bit her lips, glancing nervously at the livid marks on his neck. 'I think you're bleeding.'

'I wouldn't be surprised.' He took out a handkerchief and pressed it against his injured skin, his eyes shooting to the door as a polite knock resounded against the surface. 'My chauffeur,' he guessed, surveying the handkerchief with interest as he saw the red stain there. 'The next time we meet, I'll teach you to sheath your claws, Cat.' His smile barely camouflaged the hard certainty behind his words and they lingered afterwards as a threat or a promise.

She watched him wordlessly as he let himself out of the tack-room, unable to explain the feeling of anti-climax that gripped her. She hated Steve Lucas and she was glad he had gone! So why did it take all her vigilance to stop herself sinking back into the memory of his kisses?

CHAPTER TWO

THUNDERCLOUDS hung in the sky promising violent weather. The atmosphere was crackling with static. Cat worked in the stables grooming the horses, aware of their restlessness, feeling it answered in herself. Steve Lucas was due to return that day and Cat, for one, was not looking forward to renewing his acquaintance.

Chas had been keen to complete the purchase of Farrells while his cousin was away, warning her that things would only get tougher if Steve Lucas took over negotiations.

Spurred on by his words, Cat agreed to the terms laid down in what had previously been the draft contract, even though her solicitor, Peter Bainbridge, was away on a fishing trip and unable to tie up nameless 'details' he had mentioned on perusing Lucas-Brett's offer. As she rhythmically removed mud from Shannon's coat, she recalled Chas Lucas's words:

'Steve wants all the cottages for luxury development. He's going to have them gutted and refurbished to rent out as an extension of the manor. If you don't sign now, he'll take over and renegotiate from scratch. . .' It had been enough to make her comply. Haggling terms with Steve Lucas was something she anticipated with horror.

A prickle of awareness scratched a path up her spine to sizzle wildly at the back of her neck. She turned her head with trepidation, her eyes narrowed to meet the potent gaze of the man she least wanted to see.

'The storm's about to break.' His voice held that

prophetic calm that heralded the violent eruption of the elements. 'I don't know much about horses, but Shannon was spooked the other day by thunder. I'd take a break if I were you.'

'Thank you, Mr Lucas, I do know what I'm doing.' He had been so recently in her thoughts that she felt as if she'd conjured him up. Gathering together the brush and curry-comb, she approached him, looking up imperiously as he continued to block her way. She forced him to give way to her, although for one alarming moment she thought he was going to stay lolling in the doorway and mock her with his closeness. Fastening the stable door, she cast an eye at the heavens. He was right: the sky was as dark as night, huge thunderheads gathering over Raven's Copse to the east.

'I'll take you home. You can get changed and we'll have lunch.'

She scanned the tan suede jacket and chinos he was wearing as if his clothes would provide her with a clue to his purpose. The cream shirt he wore beneath the jacket was unfastened at the throat. Cat's eyes unwillingly noted the bronzed skin and stray silky body hair, dark against the pale material where the second button was loosened. Her eyes rose to meet his, the intoxication of her senses unconsciously provocative.

'Changed? Why should I?'

'You might like horses but I prefer you more delicately perfumed.'

'I meant, why should I come to lunch with you?' Wakening from her dream, she spoke through clenched teeth.

'Haven't we got a deal to celebrate?' His regard was steady and knowing.

Something in his manner made her extremely

uncomfortable. She felt as if she wanted to rush home and re-read her contract.

'I didn't think you had much time to waste on minor management decisions.'

'I have my humble moments.'

On the point of refusal, she hesitated. Deep in her bones she felt that Steve Lucas could still threaten the fragile security she had negotiated for her family. Why she felt that way, when everything had been officially ratified, she didn't know. Maybe having lunch would dispel the feeling. The resolution made, she still didn't feel any easier in his company. Memories of their last encounter effortlessly destroyed her composure.

'You seem tense, Catherine.'

Her shoulders stiffened, tightened to painful intensity. 'You make me tense.'

'Why?' His soft drawl was masculine and confident, as if he was playing a well-worn game.

'As you've pointed out, you're out of my league. You frighten me.'

'I find that hard to believe.' Moving ahead, he opened the door of a brand-new gold Range Rover. As he watched her, his mouth tilted into a lazy smile that for once wasn't mocking. 'You could easily bring me to my knees.'

Cat felt herself growing hot. To have his strength at her feet tangled darkly with her fantasies.

'You seem to live in those stables. Does your brother help?' he asked, sliding into the driving seat.

'He's on holiday. He's worked really hard to get to Cambridge and he hates horses.'

'I hate horses but I wouldn't let my sister support me.'

'He's only eighteen.'

'You're only nineteen.'

'How do you know?'

'I was interested, so I asked. Don't you want to go to Cambridge? Do your dreams start and end here?' His voice indicated that she had a starved imagination if she was content with her life as it was.

'I want to do what I'm doing, Mr Lucas. I have no other ambition.'

'Interesting.'

'I'm glad you think so.' She didn't want to talk about the inequalities in her family. The fact that Jamie, a year younger, had a relatively untrammelled existence while her own was strewn with worries was something she bore rather than questioned.

'You'll never get very far if you tie yourself to lame horses.'

The way that Jamie and Shannon had been bundled together in some loose metaphor said a lot about the man she was dealing with.

'And you have gone a long way, Mr Lucas.'

'My name's Steve, and I thought we'd established that I know when I'm being insulted.'

'I don't like my loyalties being treated as if they're a weakness. I don't think you can be strong unless you love people.'

'And you think I don't.'

'I think our definitions of love are very different.'

'Very probably.' He sounded bored with the subject.

Primrose Cottage came into view and Cat's tension, if possible, increased. She led the way into the cottage, aware that her companion viewed the interior decor with interest.

'Nice place,' he offered, his tone ambivalent.

Cat had always delighted in the effect of mellowness and tranquillity her home conveyed. Light furnishings contrasted with old polished wood, bright bars of light providing a contrast of brilliance and shadow. Flowers and plants proliferated, bearing witness to Jessica Farrell's love of intricate floral decoration.

'We like it.' She didn't like to dwell on the merits of the cottage, as the sunlight caught the deep azure of Steve's eyes and tainted them with avarice to Cat's supersensitive perception. Did he see the happy years that had built this home, or was he calculating the loss in profit that the Farrells' ownership would cost Lucas-Brett?

Excusing herself, she went to change for what promised to be a fraught lunch date.

When she descended the stairs, ready to go, she found Steve Lucas in conversation with her mother.

'Darling, you never told me we had a guest. Steven's mother used to live on the estate. . . Of course, that was a long time ago.'

'Over thirty years,' Steve agreed, his eyes secretive and shadowed as they met Cat's.

'I didn't know. . .' Cat was puzzled. Did Steve Lucas have some grudge against Ranleigh? Was that why he was determined to change it beyond recognition?

The slow sweep of his gaze drove such speculation from her mind. How dared he look at her like that? Cat had changed into a mint-coloured blouse with a matching pleated skirt, her dark hair a vivid contrast to the cool country colour. Her skin shone with health, sun-kissed in youthful bloom.

Steve Lucas absorbed the picture she made, aware of her chagrin, turning to compliment her mother charmingly on her home, effecting a friendly goodbye that had her parent totally disarmed. Cat was left with the disturbing impression that she had become part of something that threatened to bring havoc to her relatively uncomplicated life.

'Why did your mother leave Ranleigh?' she questioned as he seated her once more in his car.

'To go somewhere else,' was the laconic reply. Subject closed, Cat realised, her curiosity sharpened. What did Steve Lucas have to hide?

Thunder growled softly, soft thuds in the distance suggesting the storm centre was some miles away. Cat glanced up at the sky with assessing eyes. The stable lads would be on duty but she knew how the horses suffered in a storm. She would rather be at Farrells than under the scrutiny of Steve Lucas.

'Do you mind if we drive to Markham? We can have lunch at the marina.'

She was rather surprised at his choice. Markham was over forty miles away.

'We might outrun the storm,' he offered by way of an explanation.

It wasn't the storm that worried Cat. It was spending time in his company. He made her nervous. Even when he was occupied driving, he exuded masculinity from every pore. She had a fight to stop herself responding to him, seeking escape by pointedly staring out of the side window.

'You're quiet.' Steve's voice reached into her thoughts. 'Guilty conscience?'

Cat's eyes shot sideways. 'What do you mean?'

Steve took his time answering, negotiating the country road with confident assurance. 'I was teasing. Your reaction is interesting, though. What have you been up to?'

'You've only been away a matter of days. It may seem a lifetime to you but things move more slowly here.'

'Glad to hear it,' he drawled significantly. 'Seen much of Chas?'

Cat was aware of the slight difference in tone and let her gaze play over his toughly moulded profile more reflectively.

'I sold him Farrells. We were adequately chaperoned, I assure you.'

Steve smiled, his eyes still on the road and not really amused. 'So, you took notice of my warning, did you? That surprises me a little. I thought you wanted to fight.'

The way he purred the last two words left her in no doubt that the physical contact he envisaged would leave him the victor and her his willing suppliant.

'I want to get this over and done with, Mr Lucas. I have no time for your sophisticated games.'

He laughed, a soft feral laugh that made her heart beat more quickly. 'Then why did you come? The deal is signed, ratified by the UK legal department of Lucas-Brett. I have no problem accepting the price—it was within the range I'd stipulated.'

Cat was startled by his words. What game was he playing? Of course the purchase price was acceptable: it had been negotiated as part of the overall deal which guaranteed her a job managing the new stables to be built as part of the leisure complex. It also gave the Farrells an option to buy their home at the market price.

It was possible that he was unconcerned about the strings attached to the deal and was eager to tie up loose ends at Ranleigh before moving on elsewhere. But Steve Lucas didn't strike her as a man who overlooked detail. The only other possibility was that Chas had deliberately kept him in the dark. The thought made her lose colour. Had Chas gone out on a limb agreeing terms with her? If he hadn't been given the authority to accede to her demands, where did that leave Farrells?

'What's the matter? Getting cold feet? Farrells wasn't a viable prospect when Ranleigh was under new management. You really had little option but to sell.'

'It doesn't occur to you, I suppose, that I might have liked my life the way it was!' Cat played for time. She didn't underestimate this man. He would make a bad enemy.

'It's natural to resent change.' He sounded as if he came from the tough school of life. 'In a few years' time Farrells would have been near to derelict and you wouldn't have the capital to do the necessary repairs. It was an albatross around your neck. You should thank me for cutting you loose.'

'You want thanks!' She was incredulous. 'You've turned my world upside down.'

'You'll see.' His assurance was almost insulting. 'I've been down this road before. Sometimes change is for the better.'

Seething, it was on the tip of her tongue to destroy his smug confidence and tell him that the 'change' he talked about wasn't going to be quite as drastic as he thought. She held on to her temper. She would be crazy to plunge herself into needless conflict for the momentary delight of puncturing his ego.

He had given Chas the authority to complete the deal. It was hardly her problem if Chas had exceeded his instructions. That was an internal matter for Lucas-Brett. Her main concern was the contract. She had severe misgivings about signing without her solicitor's advice. If Steve Lucas didn't like what Chas had offered, any loophole would be thoroughly exploited. She could kick herself for being hustled into a hasty sale just because Steve Lucas threatened every last female cell in her body.

'Tell me about Henry Winterton? Where does he fit into the picture?'

'Henry?' She was totally thrown by the question. Henry was the vicar's son and a long-time friend. He generally escorted her when he was down from Oxford. There had never been anything serious between them. It astounded her that he should be aware of Henry at all.

'I like my women free of other obligations. You say there's nothing between you and Chas, although he doesn't see it that way. I've heard your name linked with Henry Winterton. I'm asking how serious it is.'

My women! The two words ricocheted around her mind with numbing impact. The very conceit of the man. It occurred to her that they were at cross-purposes. She had agreed to lunch because she had secretly hoped he would reassure her that the deal with Lucas-Brett was solid. His interpretation had been quite different. He thought she wanted to spend time with him!

'I can't imagine why any relationships I may have would be any business of yours, Mr Lucas,' she put matters straight. 'I don't think our last encounter left you in any doubt about my feelings. Your cut-throat attitude to those around you makes you singularly unappealing as a. . .'

'I can supply a word.'

'I don't doubt it.' She went crimson at her inability to say 'lover' with the cool assurance she desired.

'You can make as much noise as you like,' he drawled in retaliation. 'But when I kiss you, you melt. Your whole body moulds to mind, pliable, sweet and

willing. You may not like it. . .but you're not doing a
very good job of keeping away, are you?'

Cat shuddered. If only he knew how desperate she
was to avoid him! He had certainly misread her acceptance of the lunch date and yet part of what he said was
true. He inflamed her womanly instincts, bewildering
her with a host of feelings she had successfully subdued
with other men. She had been aware of sexual interest
in the past but never so blatantly or so unashamedly
expressed. Steve Lucas was different! A male animal
in the lean prime of his life and dangerous with it. The
stain of his kisses had left an indelible imprint on her
skin and, despite her fervent denials, something latent
within her responded to his spoken desires.

'Markham.' The word broke into her deep absorption and she realised that he had halted at a give-way
sign and was watching her, his blue eyes alive with
curiosity. 'I'm going to let you into a secret. When I'm
not a hot-shot businessman, I have a fatal fascination
with water.'

So it seemed. She had imagined they were to lunch
at one of the smart waterfront restaurants. Instead,
they drove to the marina basin and Steve Lucas pointed
out what he informed her was a pilot cutter initially in
service in the Bristol Channel.

'I'm supervising the refit. I have a passion for restor-
ing old boats to their former glory. I'll show you
around.'

Cat was intrigued by the cutter, a sturdy boat, with
fore and aft rigging. It had an authentic quality about
it that suggested specialised interest rather than the
white, glitzy pleasure cruiser she might have expected.
It surprised her that he should supervise the boat in
England—surely his base was in the United States?

'Chas gave me the impression you weren't intending

to spend very long at Ranleigh. This looks as if it will take some time.'

'It's nearly finished. I've been involved in several projects in Europe over the last year. Messing about on boats helps me to relax.'

It could have been coincidence that the door he opened revealed a cabin, but Cat didn't think so.

'Want to test the bunk?' He smiled slowly, easily reading her thoughts.

Moving past him, she pretended innocent compliance, sitting on the edge of the bunk and pulling down the corners of her mouth in criticism.

Steve had his arm against the door-jamb, blocking the doorway, regarding her with a lazy warmth that made her very conscious of the confined space.

'Not soft enough for you, princess?' Something about the soft purring tone and the shameless run of his eyes over her slender figure made her shift restlessly.

'I shan't be sleeping here,' she slapped him down smartly. 'How long have you been interested in boats?' Pushing herself off the bunk, Cat walked towards him, disliking his tendency to hem her in.

Steve eased to the side of the doorway so that she could go before him. The gentlemanly consideration meant that she had to brush past his body in the confined space. There was a moment that seemed to last for an eternity, when the heat and scent of their bodies mingled. Steve's chest expanded as he deliberately inhaled her essence. Cat's eyes narrowed in feline consideration and then she passed through into the corridor, shedding the intimacy of the moment into the dark pathways of the unconscious.

'I used to have a lot of hobbies as a boy,' he answered her question, willing to act out her rules of engagement. 'I was alone a lot. We moved rooms more times than I can remember. I started building cheap models to pass the time. . . Now I've graduated to the real thing.'

Cat frowned. The Lucas family were old money. That didn't suggest a deprived childhood. Was he spinning her a line to soften her up?

'Rooms?' She queried. 'I thought the Lucas family all lived in mansions. Was your father the black sheep of the family?'

He gave her a level look, bleak enlightenment shadowing his features before a smile camouflaged his feelings and he shrugged.

'Chas must be more discreet than I thought. Let's just say my childhood wasn't quite as comfortable as his.'

Cat was curious. There seemed to be more than one skeleton in Steve Lucas's past. He clearly didn't want to elaborate on the subject and she stifled her interest, determined not to give him the satisfaction of accusing her of prying. Moving on, she completed the tour of the boat.

'What do you think of her?' Steve Lucas smiled at her absorption.

'It's interesting to find you think something of the past worth saving.' Cat met his eyes, her own a broil of dark emotion.

'I'm saving Ranleigh. There were other companies interested that would make me look like the Heritage Society.'

Cat found this hard to believe and her expression was most revealing.

'Tell me what you have planned for the future. You'll need finance if you want to open a similar business.'

If she needed proof that he was ignorant of the significant clauses of the contract negotiated by his cousin, she had it! From his manner, she gathered that he might even be considering acting as her financial advisor, a thinly disguised gesture of goodwill to romance her into bed.

Watching him go to the compact fridge, she saw him retrieve a bottle of white wine, busying himself with opening it. In the face of a direct question Cat found herself unable to lie. She had intended to quiz Chas before putting her cards on the table but she had no intention of conspiring in any attempt at deceit.

'I'm going to manage the new stables at Ranleigh when they're built. Didn't Chas tell you?'

He turned, his expression non-comprehending. 'Stables? What stables?' His eyes narrowed to cold blue chips of ice. 'Nothing in the plans stipulates stables! And if they did, I wouldn't employ a nineteen-year-old girl to run them.'

Hackles rising at his blatantly sexist attitude, Cat was glad to have the issue out in the open.

'It was agreed in the initial draft that I would manage a newly sited stable belonging to the Ranleigh complex. I merely agreed to the terms offered by your company.'

Steve Lucas laughed cynically as if he couldn't believe what he was hearing. 'Let me get this right. For the pleasure of buying you out, Chas has agreed to build you a brand-new stable and given you the job as manager. Dream on, sweetheart, it just isn't going to happen.'

Coal-black eyes were militant. 'You have to, other-wise you'll be in breach of contract. Your company approached me, Mr Lucas. I was quite happy to run Farrells and live on the estate. You wanted my land. Money wasn't the main issue. I'm talking about belong-ing, tradition, the fabric of life you can only scratch at by buying pieces of the past like this boat.'

'Well, listen to you.' His tone silkened and slashed. 'There's a tradition as old as time that makes men part with their senses to please a pretty girl. Did you sleep with Chas to keep your little corner of old England?'

Her hand whipped to his face but he caught it in painful collision. She yelped and found herself bound by his strength, her wrist captured in his, her face turned mutinously away in denial of his retribution.

'He must have rocks in his head if you didn't. What else did he promise you? You might as well tell me,' his voice hissed next to her ear. 'I'll find out soon enough.'

Fear mingled with angry frustration. Cat felt as if she had entered a nightmare. 'The contract ensures we have the option to buy the cottage. All we want is to continue as we were before. It's our home, can't you understand that?'

She was incensed by the turn of events. What sort of company was it that had one executive making a deal and another furiously repudiating it?

'What I understand, sweetheart, is that you've got a substantial amount of money without planning to give up anything for it. All you've lost is the dubious pleasure of worrying about Farrells' finances. You expect me to house you, employ you, swell your bank balance and think I've got a good deal. That cottage alone is worth over fifty thousand a year in rental. Well, I've got news for you.' He pushed her arms behind her back, bringing her into the warmth of his body, his blue eyes ranging over her face. 'I'm offering jobs and paying compensation on the estate because I don't like bad publicity when I open a new venture. Edward Ranleigh didn't leave any stipulations regarding those on the estate. As far as he was concerned, his duties died with him. I don't like making people homeless but that hardly applies to you. You can find a new home in comfort wherever you like, so don't expect me to baby you.' Letting her go, he poured the wine down the sink.

'I don't think either of us is hungry. Shall we go?'

Cat rubbed her wrists, feeling the blood tingling back through her veins, watching him warily. He was furious and past reasoning with.

Could he break the contract she had made with Chas? Clearly he had enough money not to worry about the expense of lawyers, but would he expend energy breaking a deal made by one of his own executives? Chas was his cousin and he would certainly be put in a humiliating position if Steve Lucas used his own legal department to destroy a contract they themselves had drawn up and sanctioned.

She was escorted from the pilot cutter like a stowaway being marched to shore. Several heads were raised in the boatyard, greetings stilled on their lips at the expression on Steve Lucas's face.

'Will you stop manhandling me!' Cat tried to pull her arm free. 'I'd prefer to find my own way home!'

'Not on your life.' His expression raked her contemptuously. 'I'm not letting you get on the hotline to Chas. He'll be on the next plane to New York before you had the chance to replace the phone. My cousin has a neat way of avoiding his responsibilities.'

'You don't have to shackle me like a prisoner!' She pulled at his grasp on her jacket, his fingers pinching her skin painfully.

'What do you expect, if you get involved in fraudulent deals to milk a multinational company? If Chas wasn't Frank Lucas's grandson, you'd lose more than a little dignity, darling.'

'Fraudulent!' she squeaked, her outrage making her

swivel and direct a kick at his ankle. 'Take that back! It was nothing of the sort. . .'

She gave him a hasty glance when he winced and half lifted her the rest of the way. A family crossing the car park gave them a curious look but they were too involved in their battle to take any notice.

Cat went hot with panic when he pressed her against the Range Rover, anchoring her with his body while he freed the lock. The overwhelming maleness he possessed made her skin break out in tiny beads of sweat, her hands pushing against the hard wall of his chest, the angry heave of bone and muscle immovable. He moved so that his thigh was across hers, a fleeting flicker of his lashes registering the intimacy. Cat felt her whole body blush. In the short time she had known him, she had come into physical collision with him frequently and it was intensely disturbing.

'Get in!' he instructed grittily, almost folding her into the seat before coming around the car, watching her like a hawk the whole of the time.

'Will you stop treating me like a criminal?' she raged. 'It's not my fault Chas has offered terms you don't like. Speak to him! You said you wanted the deal closing. I was hardly likely to refuse a decent offer. Business, after all, is business.'

'Yeah?' He turned on the ignition, his scowl black and uncompromising. 'So why did you come out with me today? Don't tell me you thought I'd celebrate Lucas-Brett's being taken to the cleaners. It seems to me you've done a good job on Chas and you thought you'd smooth out any complications. . .like me being as mad as hell,' he growled furiously.

She had no answer to that one. She had agreed to lunch because she wanted to reassure herself he wasn't going to threaten her family's security. Steve Lucas hung over her like a doom crow, a dark, dangerous presence unsettling and wrecking her peace of mind.

'I think Chas has his own axe to grind. But you must know more about that than me.' She made a stab in the dark and felt a sear of blue fire sweep her features.

'And what's that supposed to mean?' he asked, his voice forced into an even tone.

'I'm just guessing.' Cat studied his profile with growing certainty. His jaw tensed, irritation evident on his lean features. 'But I'm right, aren't I?'

He didn't reply, ramming the gears home with suppressed violence. Whatever he was thinking had certainly got under his skin.

'What are you going to do?' Cat found his grim silence unnerving. She wanted to know if his anger was prophetic of a battle ahead or if he was merely indulging his temper because things hadn't gone his way.

'I think I'll let you stew on that.' He smiled evilly. 'But I can assure you, you'll hear more on the subject. And when you do, you won't find it pleasant.'

Cat glared at him frustratedly. She needed to see her solicitor. She had a dreadful sense of foreboding. The contract had looked watertight to her untrained eye but she had become all too aware of the pitfalls of signing without legal advice.

What on earth had Chas been up to? Steve thought they were lovers in collusion against him, but that was nonsense. So why had Chas pretended a relationship that didn't exist? And why had he hurried her into a deal he knew his cousin would try to break?

It occurred to Cat that she had become involved in something deeper than boyish rivalry. Chas had challenged the leader of the pack in more than his clumsy attempt to thwart him over the stables. The friendly, seemingly ingenuous charm of Steve Lucas's cousin had entangled her in intrigue. She was only beginning dimly to comprehend that it went deeper than a business deal—something much more fundamental was at stake!

CHAPTER THREE

'REALLY, my dear, you should never have signed anything until I had time to go through it. The purchase price is safe enough but the building of new premises is not tied down. Lucas-Brett could delay for years and then plead lack of demand for the idea. What this contract says is that, if they should build the stables, you will be offered the manager's job.' Peter Bainbridge, the family solicitor, was sympathetic but clearly thought the time for effective consultation had passed.

Cat's eyes smarted with disappointment. 'And the cottage. What about that?'

'Again,' he sighed, 'you say you'll pay the market price for the house. . .but when? If Lucas-Brett drag their heels, the market price of the property within the grounds of an exclusive leisure park will go sky-high. You may not be able to meet the price.' Peter Bainbridge was clearly embarrassed at the bad news he had to convey. 'You have a good reputation, Miss Farrell. I'm sure you'll be able to start again. After all, you're a proven businesswoman. Keeping Farrells profitable took a good deal of effort and ingenuity. . .'

Cat listened absently to her solicitor but her mind was seething with troubles. Steve Lucas didn't have to do a thing, merely play delaying tactics. No doubt he was having a good laugh at her expense. She wondered at Chas's duplicity. Had he rushed her into a quick deal, aware of the pitfalls in the contract? Certainly, he had had the benefit of his own lawyers to fall back on.

Leaving the solicitor's office, she decided to walk back to Ranleigh, needing time to think out her next move. Hours ago, she had provoked Steve Lucas into a steaming temper. Now it looked as if she was the one who had been well and truly duped.

Cat returned to Primrose Cottage, poignantly aware of its timeless beauty. She had the onerous task of ringing around her customers to give them notice of the stables closing. She had negotiated eight weeks' leeway for that, another factor that wouldn't endear her to Steve Lucas. She didn't mention the problems of the day to her mother or Jamie, not wanting to worry them before she had to.

She had just put down the receiver, after ringing her tenth customer, when the telephone rang, making her jump with shock.

'Catherine?' A familiar voice made her sit up straight, unaccountably blushing. She was glad he couldn't see her.

'What do you want?' she asked churlishly.

'I think you'd better come over to Ranleigh. I have something I want to discuss with you.'

Cat frowned suspiciously. 'Anything you wish to discuss can be done over the phone. I don't enjoy your character assassinations or your company——'

'Be here in half an hour or I'll come and get you.' The phone went dead and Cat pulled a face at it.

Wearily, she pushed a hand through her dark hair. She supposed she had little choice. If there was the slightest chance Steve Lucas would honour the spirit of the agreement she had made, then she had to respond to it. Certainly she would get nowhere antagonising him.

Crossing the estate, she made her way to Ranleigh. The door of the manor house was wedged open and the sound of workmen could be heard on approach. Paint and wood-shavings had taken the musty smell away from the hallway.

'Is Mr Lucas here?' she asked one of the men.

'Upstairs. Both of them. I'd keep well clear if I was you.'

Frowning, she soon realised what the man had meant. The voices were indistinguishable from below but, upon mounting the stairs, it became clear a heated argument was taking place. The closer she got, the sounds shaped themselves into words and most of the talking was being done by Steve Lucas.

'I suppose this is another attempt to get home quick. I'd oblige you if I hadn't promised your grandfather to turn you into a businessman.'

'You wanted the deal sewn up,' Chas retaliated. 'How were you going to do it? Cat wouldn't sell without some deal over the house and stables——'

'So you decided to play fairy godmother and grant her three wishes.'

'No, I——'

'No!' The word was condemning. 'You left holes in the contract I could drive a bus through. Lucas-Brett isn't some cowboy outfit. The Press would love this—a nineteen-year-old girl being steam-rollered by corporate heavyweights. It's an unholy mess!'

Cat cleared her throat, causing both men to look in her direction.

'You wanted to see me?' She felt as if she were standing on the edge of a volcano. Steve Lucas's words made her a little more optimistic about a compromise being reached, but she couldn't see him capitulating completely.

'Come in.' Steve was expansive, his mockery cutting. Chas looked down at his shoes, like a small boy being chastised by his headmaster. 'Where have you been? I've been trying to get hold of you all afternoon.'

Memories of their earlier encounter hung in the air between them. 'I went to see my solicitor.'

'And?'

'I think you know what he told me.' Dark eyes leaden, she bore his harsh gaze bravely.

'Why didn't you consult him before you signed?' Steve glanced from one to the other. 'Come on, I want to know!'

'He was away over the weekend,' Cat informed him, her lashes veiling her eyes. All her misgivings about rushing things through while her solicitor was away came back to haunt her.

'So why didn't you wait?'

The silence was killing.

'I told Cat you wouldn't offer such a good deal as the original draft agreement,' Chas owned up. 'She was only trying to get the best deal for her family. You can't blame her for that.'

Steve didn't look convinced. 'I'd scent a conspiracy if I thought you had two brain-cells to rub together. Between you, you've managed to place Lucas-Brett in an extremely difficult position.' Raking his fingers through his hair, he looked thoughtful. 'You can go, Chas,' he said in aside without looking at his cousin.

'Oh, no!' Chas got to his feet but stood his ground. 'This is between you and me. Cat is just an innocent bystander!'

'I'm taking over all future negotiations. I really don't see how you can help.' The soft, vicious tone made Cat wince. Chas's position confused her. He seemed to have sold her down the river and now he was defending her.

The younger man coloured darkly. 'Don't pretend it's business. I've seen the way you look at her——'

'Then you should feel very proud of yourself for putting her at my mercy. Get out of here before I throw you out.'

Chas swallowed thickly, clearly conscience-stricken. 'If he hadn't found out about the deal, I would have honoured it. You have to believe that, Cat——'

'I said go!' Steve Lucas moved forward and Chas gave way, moving towards the door.

'I'll see you later,' he promised Cat, before eyeing his muscle-bound cousin and retreating rapidly.

There was a short silence when he had gone. Chas's words electrified the space between them. Cat was an independent spirit. The idea that a predator like Steve Lucas could take hold of her life and mould it at will challenged everything she held dear.

'We have something of a dilemma here.' His voice recalled the lethal poise of a snake before it struck. 'What am I going to do about you? Stables might not be a bad idea but they're certainly not a priority. Meanwhile you're squatting in a relatively expensive property.'

'We'd be willing to buy the cottage,' Cat maintained doggedly. 'It does mean an awful lot to us.'

'Maybe it's not for sale,' he returned provocatively.

'Are you doing this for sadistic amusement?' she fired up. 'Or is there some point? What do you want, Steve?'

Those enticing blue eyes mocked and beckoned. 'I want persuading, Catherine.'

Spine ramrod-straight, Cat gave him a blistering look. 'That's the most insulting thing anyone has ever said to me. Who do you think you are, Steve Lucas? Whatever you believe, I have never cheapened myself to give a man sexual favours to gain what I want. And I don't intend to start now!'

Steve laughed, unmoved by her protestations. 'I'm afraid you're in the grown-up league now, sweetheart, but I wasn't suggesting you sell yourself cheaply. You can't have any scruples about getting rid of Chas. He's got a pretty little heiress languishing back home. She'd make him an excellent wife; you wouldn't.'

'Not enough money, I take it.' She closed in on him, a terrible desire to lash out at him seizing her.

'I don't think any man would value a wife who was willing to sleep with his cousin.'

The sound of the slap ricocheted from wall to wall, leaving white marks on Steve Lucas's face. Steve very effectively imprisoned her wrists and swung her around until she was pinned against the wall with her hands above her head.

'Such passion.' His breathing was a little uneven, male excitement heightening at her feeble defence.

'If it's hate you want,' she panted angrily, 'you have exclusive rights.'

'Shame, Catherine.' His silky voice mocked her. 'It's a lot more complicated than hate.'

Cat twisted desperately, knowing what close proximity to Steve Lucas could do to her. His body heat lured her senses, the force of his personality beating down her resolve to resist him.

'Can't you find any willing victims, Steve?' Cat taunted, knowing her silk polo-neck was revealing the taut curves of her breasts.

Steve merely let his gaze examine the beauty of her face, seeming fascinated by the jet-black hair and eyebrows, the dark eyes fringed by equally dark lashes, the smooth skin that covered high cheekbones and the full, generous lips that tempted him mercilessly. His blue eyes considered her with sexual intent.

'I'll sell you the cottage.' Bending his head, he let his mouth move over her cheek in a lazy caress.

Cat was consumed by his body heat, the musky scent of him triggering her responses. His mouth drew fiery patterns over her skin, the arch of her body away from the wall finding the hard bulk of his and dissolving inside with the effect of the collision.

'I'll set you up in business——'

'I know what you're suggesting!' She twisted away, frantic to break his hypnotic spell. 'I'd rather be homeless and starve. Get off me!'

Laughing softly, Steve Lucas released her and moved away. 'Don't panic, honey. . . Just testing.'

Pouring himself a drink, he waved a careless hand at the silver tray crammed with bottles. 'Can I get you something?'

'No!' She felt near to tears. A muscle tensed in his jaw, his eyes serious as he took in her distress.

'I think you need a brandy.' Pouring her one, he brought it to her, keeping a measured distance. 'You're more dangerous than I thought. You've got me feeling guilty.'

Sipping her drink, she winced as the raw spirit burnt her throat. 'I don't understand any of this. Chas seems to have deliberately misled me and then——'

'Chas got cold feet because he likes you. So he drew up a contract which could go either way just to cause maximum irritation. He's hoping I'll send him home. I have the dubious task of making a businessman out of him,' he informed her, looking as if the task galled him very much. 'Chas is very good at messing things up, so sabotaging a deal was right up his street. Of course he won't admit it. He has a doting mother and grandfather to keep sweet. His grandfather is president of Lucas-Brett and one of the major shareholders in the company. I owe him a lot, so I'm stuck with Chas.' Pausing, he touched his glass to hers. 'It looks as if I'm stuck with you as well.'

Wide-eyed, she regarded him apprehensively. 'What do you mean?'

He didn't answer. 'Tell me why the cottage is so important.'

Cat was deeply suspicious of his motives. From the very beginning their relationship had been antagonistic. He had called her a gold-digger, accused her of using her body to further her own ends. It was the first time he had openly asked her to explain her feelings about leaving her home.

She gave him the bare bones of the situation. How her mother wasn't in the best of health and wouldn't hear of living elsewhere. How the Farrells had been at Ranleigh for over a hundred years and that her brother Jamie found the idea of leaving just as unbearable.

'And what about you?' Steve Lucas queried with surprising gentleness at the end of her explanation. 'You're the one trying to hold this whole thing together but you rarely mention yourself in all this.'

'It's hard to imagine any other existence,' she admitted honestly. 'I've been in charge of the stables for three years, although my mother had to sign things before I reached eighteen. Even before my father died, I always helped. It was a natural progression.'

'It sounds as if you didn't have much choice. . . unlike Jamie.'

Cat's eyes flashed at the implied criticism. 'I always loved horses. I wanted to be world champion, ride in the Olympics, it was a wonderful life. . .'

She was unaware of the clarity of her own enthusiasm. Cat drew a picture of a life that had a sense of continuity regardless of ambition. She had an uninhibited joy in the life she had chosen. She had grown up at Ranleigh, her father owning a stables—many a young girl's dream. She had followed her own personal star ever since.

'And I've spoilt it?'

'Yes. . . No. No one's to blame. Things change, don't they?'

'Yes,' he agreed from his vantage point, leaning against the mantelpiece. 'Things change.'

There was a silence between them. Steve Lucas rested his eyes on her face, his own contemplative. He was miles away, remembering a time when he had wanted to gather his past to him to find some direction for the future. He was as steeped in memories as she was, but they afforded no security blanket for him and never would.

'The business world is tough. Being able to take over the reins of an established business is one thing, adapting to changing circumstances is another thing entirely.' Suddenly he was a businessman looking over a fledgling project. 'I'd need to know there was a demand for a stables to be added to the Ranleigh complex. Horses can't be stored away until they're needed: they have to be fed and maintained, and veterinary bills aren't cheap.'

'But——'

'How can you find out if there's a market before we open club membership? You tell me.' With the air of a man who knew all the answers, he waited for her reply.

'Well. . .' She frowned, thinking hard. 'Lucas-Brett must have done some market research. I could start there.'

'Oh.' The mock air of enlightenment was crushing. 'And why should the company hand over expensive market research material to you?'

Storm clouds gathered in Cat's dark eyes. 'If you're trying to say the whole thing is impossible, I'd rather you just said it. I'm sure I can find some compensation for my family elsewhere.'

'Meaning?'

'Meaning I won't leave Ranleigh without a fight. If that means having to expose your company's business practices to the Press, then I'll do it!'

Cat restrained a shudder at the thought. She had thought he'd softened towards her when she had revealed her family's dilemma. Now she knew it was nothing so benign. Steve Lucas had been on a fact-finding mission. He wanted to know just how deeply rooted a problem the Farrells represented.

Pushing himself away from the mantelpiece, he regarded her challengingly. 'So you do want to fight?' The words were soft with menace and Cat felt her resolve weaken momentarily.

'I have no choice, Mr Lucas.' Her voice was firm and she held her head high, drawing on inner reserves of strength she hadn't known she possessed.

'I'll give you a choice.' He sauntered over to where she stood, his body relaxed and fluid compared to the rigid lines of her own. 'I'll think about adding the stables to the project if I'm convinced you have the organisational skills to run them.'

Cat's lashes flickered, surprise and suspicion showing fleetingly on her expressive features. 'And how do I prove that?' she queried, not in the least taken in by his sudden olive branch.

'It's quite simple.' The triumphant gleam in those blue eyes told her she wouldn't like what was to come.

'From tomorrow morning you're my personal assistant with a salary commensurate with that guaranteed in the contract for managing the stables. Your brother Jamie can help at Farrells in your place. If he has any problems with that, he can come and see me.'

Cat stifled a yelp of horror. He had neatly turned the tables on her. He knew she would dread the idea of daily contact with him and was expecting her to refuse. If she did, he could claim that she had turned down employment with Lucas-Brett during the interim period before the stables were built.

'Why don't you sleep on it?' he suggested silkily. 'I start work at seven. If you wish to take up employment with Lucas-Brett, be here in the morning——' his gaze swept her jeans and sweatshirt '—appropriately dressed.'

Cat refused to give him the satisfaction of showing her frustrated anger. She felt like howling into the night but instead she promised in a flat emotionless tone to consider the idea.

His mocking, 'Until tomorrow,' echoed in her head as she left Ranleigh Manor and followed the path back to Primrose Cottage. The deal she had made with Lucas-Brett had turned into a nightmare. Cat had little doubt there was worse to come. . .

The next morning, Cat viewed herself in the mirror. She had never worked in an office and had no idea what the job of a personal assistant involved. It sounded like one of those Girl Friday roles. She had a vague image of a girl in a grey suit and big glasses, the universal gofer.

Matching a cream blazer with a coffee-coloured blouse and skirt, she walked along the estate path, pondering on the twists of fate. In three days, she had

bargained and bartered for the future of her family and
now she hung in limbo having to earn the respect of a
man whom, she suspected, had every intention of
proving her an incompetent idiot.

Jamie had been stirring on her departure. He had
not taken kindly to having his holidays curtailed and
she had been forced to impart to him something of
their troubles. It had been a relief to share her worries
and Jamie had agreed to help, gloomily reflecting that
his friend Gavin was coming to stay but not seriously
making any objections.

Steve Lucas was on the phone when she walked into
his office at Ranleigh. He acknowledged her with a
brief nod, pointing towards the coffee and pushing his
cup forward for a refill.

She viewed it mutinously for a moment and then
stiffly picked it up and obeyed his request, replacing
the cup in front of him and sitting in a chair at the
opposite side of his desk.

'Get yourself some,' he ordered, his hand briefly
covering the mouthpiece, watching her as she did so,
catching the flare of her eyes as she returned to her
seat and noticed his interest.

He surveyed the length of her legs, bare of stockings,
and contemplated how she still managed to look like a
gypsy in formal clothes. She was screaming resistance
from every pore. He knew she had turned up that
morning to flout his attempt to outwit her and reluctantly admired her for it.

Concluding his business, he replaced the receiver,
attempting a professional tone. 'Can you type?'

'No.'

'No office skills?'

'I can't type or do shorthand and wouldn't know one

end of a photocopier from another. Not everyone desires to be a secretary, Mr Lucas.'

'I forgot. You've spent your life cleaning up after horses—very upwardly mobile.'

'I wasn't——'

'Being a snob? It never crossed my mind.' Resplendent in a white shirt with maroon silk tie, the jacket of his suit hanging over the back of his chair, he looked virile and vital, very much the businessman.

'OK. Well, something you can do. I want you to spend the morning calling various stables in the area and finding places for the horses at Farrells. I can't wait eight weeks to demolish something that can be dealt with in a day.' His mouth curled into a wince of a smile. 'Much as it pains me, Lucas-Brett will foot the bill.'

'But I promised eight weeks' notice——'

'Sure you did. So you offer the same cost for the first month and a month's free bed and breakfast. I'm sure no one will object.' He dealt with her scruples as if she were severely lacking in ingenuity. 'And Catherine——' he stopped her in her tracks '—I said bed and breakfast, not the honeymoon suite at the Savoy. You're costing me enough.'

Cat's temper hit boiling point. Marching back to his desk, she placed her hands on it, her eyes hot cauldrons of fire.

'Is there one dot or comma on that contract that you intend to honour? What does eight weeks matter in a history as long as Ranleigh's? Are you such a cold-hearted materialist you can't see what you do to people?'

He rose slowly until his blue eyes were on level with hers. A will as hard as granite smashed her protest to smithereens. 'Get real and get going! Otherwise you won't even register with Personnel.'

Cat jerked back as if she had been bitten.

'You have a job to do, Miss Farrell. I suggest you get on with it.'

Cat left his office in shock. At this rate Farrells would be a memory by the end of the week!

It was a demonically constructed punishment to make her the instrument of winding up the family business. True, she had the contacts and knew her customers, but every booking confirmed was a nail in Farrells' coffin.

It didn't take her long to realise that she was woefully inadequate in her role as personal assistant. In between her own calls, she had a host of incoming lines on the switchboard. She was getting hopelessly harassed, cutting people off, when Steve Lucas roared from his office and gave her a crash course in how to be a receptionist.

'You put them on hold, like this.' He flicked the board with arrogant accomplishment. 'Then you enquire whether I want to speak to them. If I don't, you think up some excuse that sounds plausible,' he stressed, clearly doubting her powers of invention. 'Got that?'

'Thank you.'

Her stilted answer spoke volumes, but he chose to ignore countless chapters and grunted, 'Good.'

Altogether, Cat considered, she saw too much of him. It was like living with the man. When he wandered through to the reception area while she was on the phone, she regarded him through narrowed eyes.

This time he seemed to be merely stretching his legs. When the threat of direct confrontation was allayed, she found herself taking in his appearance with avid curiosity.

His dark hair was styled in fashionable slick perfection that spoke of a top-rank stylist. She doubted if he was consciously vain—more likely he had someone to make him appointments, counting on them to choose a professional image for a corporate whiz-kid. His eyebrows, she noted, were straight for the most part, tilting up slightly as they neared the bridge of his nose.

She was surprised to hear him talking in a rapid expressionless monotone before she caught sight of the dictaphone. Letters and reports for some office robot who presumably knew how to type and managed not to send the photocopier into a state of trauma. One hand eased his thigh and she watched with an unconscious fascination, momentarily losing her thread and not hearing the piping enquiry from the other end of the line.

Some fatal travesty of timing brought Steve's eyes to hers and for a moment the office routine dissolved into a transparent charade and she was caught in a fantasy of blue, trapped in a web that she had foolishly helped to spin.

Steve cleared his throat. Cat blushed brilliantly and went into a rapid explanation of terms that the bewildered person on the other end of the line had already heard. The experience left her emotionally shattered long after Steve had returned to his office. With a glance he could tear into her thoughts and steal them from her.

Chas caught up with her during her lunch break. She was sitting behind her desk, taking a desultory interest in a cheese sandwich.

'Can we talk?' he asked sheepishly. 'I called in at the stables but your brother said you were over here. Jamie said you were working for Steve! I could hardly believe my ears.'

'I'm having problems believing it myself.' Her expression was leaden and not encouraging. 'He's in there if you want him.'

Chas squirmed uncomfortably under the accusation he saw in her eyes. Casting a glance at the half-open doorway, he was relieved to see his cousin occupied on the phone.

'Let me take you to dinner tonight. I'd like a chance to explain. I really am sorry things turned out the way they have.'

'I don't think that would be a very good idea,' she began, not wishing Farrells' deal to get any worse.

'Come to the Swan with me. Please, Cat. I think you need to know a bit more about your new boss, for your own sake.'

Her dark lashes flickered to shield her eyes from his earnest gaze. Curiosity, together with a healthy sense of self-preservation, won out.

'All right. But don't pick me up at the cottage. I'll meet you at the pub.'

'Catherine!' a familiar voice bellowed from the inner sanctum.

'See you later.' Chas made a hasty retreat and Cat got up stiffly, not used to being one of Steve Lucas's minions, and long-sufferingly trudged into his office to obey his summons.

The man in question was sprawled in his chair, his hair ruffled, his tie pulled away from his collar, and was busily detaching a gold cuff-link.

'I don't pay you to gossip,' he grouched without looking up. 'Who were you talking to?'

'Your cousin,' she supplied, suspecting he knew already. 'Would you like a progress report?'

The short laugh was insulting and she felt her fingers curl into her palms, the nails inflicting moon shapes on her skin. 'I was talking about the stables.'

'Of course you were.' Cuff-link removed, he began to roll back his sleeve. 'So. . .?' A flash of cobalt seared her. Whatever demonic instinct had prompted him to invite her into his office, he seemed to be regretting it.

'I've placed six of the horses and two ponies. I think I can close Farrells in two weeks, no sooner than that.'

'I can live with that.' Beginning a similar ritual on his second cuff-link, he flicked her with his gaze. 'If you were a secretary, you'd offer to help.'

'I'm afraid I've never seen myself pampering a man for my wages.' The words slipped out, and Cat found herself biting her lip, caught between nervous laughter and real dread.

'Oh, Catherine,' he intoned deeply, 'you have an awful lot to learn about pampering a man.' With his savage tug, the cuff-link flipped across the room, his cuff torn, his eyes brilliant with a frustration Cat didn't understand.

'What did Chas want?' he growled, barely maintaining a civil tone.

'He'd heard from Jamie that I was working for you. He seemed surprised.'

Steve studied her remorselessly, watching the different emotions of fear, outrage and resentment chase each other across her beautiful features.

'More likely trying to ingratiate himself after leaving you to face the rap the other night.'

Cat found herself rising to Chas's defence. 'You made it difficult for him to stay.'

'Poor Chas,' he mourned without an ounce of sincerity. 'Full of pretty speeches and self-interest.'

Cat eyed him with dislike. 'At least he makes pretty speeches,' she muttered under her breath.

'You can go, Miss Farrell. I'd suggest an early night, with a book. We'll be busy tomorrow.'

Feeling that she loathed every inch of him, she didn't dare reply. She strongly suspected that he knew everything about her rendezvous with Chas. But what did that matter? He had no right to dictate whom she saw in her free time. Besides, she needed to know what was going on. And for that she was prepared to run the gauntlet of Steve Lucas's anger and the possible consequences that followed.

CHAPTER FOUR

THE Swan was a country pub without the affectation that adorned inner city replicas. Sketches of Royal Windsor, Ranleigh and other historical stately homes were displayed with pride on every wall.

Chas Lucas and Cat Farrell were tucked away in one of the alcove recesses, talking in lowered voices like fugitives with a guilty secret.

'I'm sorry you have to get involved with this,' Chas fretted, his eyes gloomy. 'I know it looks as if I was taking advantage of your lack of business experience but the legal department would have been on the hotline to Steve straight away if I hadn't pretended I was leaving the company's options open by not tying us down to anything concrete. I intended to follow through on the deal. . .' He faltered at the straight look she gave him. 'OK, I knew there was a possibility Steve would find out. I wanted to get home quickly. . . I expected him to kick me back across the Atlantic and cut his losses over Farrells. I didn't think he'd take it out on you. I should have figured on him being bloody-minded about the whole thing.'

Cat wondered at his naïveté. Her own brief acquaintance with Steve Lucas led her to believe that anyone foolish enough to challenge him would get a very raw deal.

'Why didn't you tell me?' Cat regarded him with exasperation. 'You may have a grudge against your cousin but it's my life you're messing around with. You hurried me into signing a contract that could leave my family in a disastrous situation. If Steve wants to be ruthless about it, he could take Farrells at a bargain basement price——'

'He won't do that,' Chas interrupted hastily, impressed by the angry frustration in her eyes. 'He doesn't like the deal but he doesn't want any bad publicity——'

'If you think I'm going to expose my stupidity to the Press, you're very much mistaken. I have some pride!' Cat was incensed.

'Yes, well, we both know that but I wouldn't broadcast it, if I were you. They're a powerful weapon, the media, and this isn't the time to get principled about the whole thing.'

'Heaven forbid.' She was chill.

'I'm sorry, Cat. I wish I'd never involved you in this, but now it's done we have to be practical. Steve feels a moral obligation to honour the contract but he's not going to make it easy for you. He's not sure of your part in all this and we do have the. . .er—other complication as well.'

'Complication?' She blushed fiery red.

'Exactly.' Chas frowned. 'I tried to make him back off, pretending you were my girlfriend, but that backfired. It just convinced him you were on the make.'

'I wanted to talk to you about that. . .' She broke off as the door of the public house opening made her look up. Cold dread swept over her as she met a pair of freezing blue eyes.

Penelope Cheetham accompanied Steve Lucas, her bright chatter making up for the silence of the other three protagonists.

'This place is getting popular all of a sudden. Slumming, darling?' She smiled a welcome at Cat and Chas but the comment was addressed to Steve Lucas.

'I like a touch of local colour. You don't mind if we join you, do you?' It wasn't a question and Cat exchanged a glance with Chas that bespoke mutual horror.

A neat blonde with green eyes, Penelope was elegant and sophisticated. The slight widening of her eyes at Cat showed she wasn't totally oblivious to the atmosphere but she camouflaged it well.

'Can I get anyone a drink?' Steve's smooth tones sounded easy and relaxed. Cat knew he was furious, which made her as taut as a bowstring.

Her eyes followed him to the bar. A soft suede jacket clothed his broad shoulders, his dark hair brushing the collar, his profile harsh.

'Hands off.' Penny rapped her knuckles with a beer mat, causing Cat to drag her gaze back to the table. Chas had turned away, exchanging a few words with one of the workmen from the estate.

'I'm sorry?' She frowned, her perplexed expression drawing a vinegary smile.

'You will be, darling.' Penelope Cheetham swept a glance over her raven-haired rival. Cat Farrell, in her little-girl tunic jumper and fun-print skirt, might not be dressed to kill but she created a colourful contrast, her striking colouring effortlessly exotic. Her careless chic had been almost amusing when she was totally unconscious of her own beauty. But something told the older woman that young Cat was growing up.

Aware of the muted hostility that had replaced the other woman's glossy superiority, Cat wondered what she'd done to upset her. The 'hands off' remark sounded as though Penny was making a claim on Steve Lucas. They had entered the Swan together but that could have been coincidence. There hadn't been much time for Penny to get acquainted, Cat reflected. Steve had spent most of his time hounding her.

It was a difficult evening. Sticking solidly to orange juice, Cat made a point of not allowing her senses to be clouded by alcohol. Penelope Cheetham slipped back into the role of vivacious socialite as soon as Steve rejoined them, chatting about mutual friends on the show-jumping circuit, and asked whether Cat was to enter the Maurier Cup.

'My father's just bought a decent thoroughbred called Blood Star. He won't let me near him—says the horse is too much for a woman. I think you could handle him, Cat. Do you want me to have a word?'

Confused by Penny's inconsistencies, Cat was about to say she'd be interested to view the horse but would bow to Colonel Cheetham's judgement, when Steve Lucas stepped in and made her eyes flare with mutiny.

'Catherine works for me now. I like my staff fully operational and preferably in one piece.'

'She must have spare time, darling. Whatever is it that you do, Cat? You must have hidden talents to become so invaluable to Lucas-Brett.'

Steve smiled thinly. 'She's my personal assistant.'

'Really? How glamorous.' That Penelope Cheetham didn't like that particular piece of news showed in the tightening of her mouth. 'What a clever girl you are.'

'Not really. I'm winding up Farrells at the moment. Steve felt I was the best person for the job.'

Chas looked appalled but his cousin remained unperturbed.

'Catherine knows the estate. I've often found it useful to have someone in on the ground floor. It prevents misunderstandings.'

'It must.' Penelope Cheetham's thinly disguised irony brought horrified comprehension to Cat's dark eyes. Steve Lucas might intend to punish her by making her work daily for him but, as far as the local grapevine went, the implication put upon their closeness would be entirely different.

Eventually the evening came to an end. Cat rose to her feet with the others, grateful that she would soon be able to escape her new boss's hateful presence. But even in that she was thwarted.

'Why don't you give Penny a lift back to Cheetham's, Chas? I see you've brought your car. I'll walk back with Cat. I feel like some fresh air.'

Put like that, no one could object. Cat felt as if she had been publicly branded. The last thing she wanted was to walk the mile and a half to Ranleigh with Steve Lucas. As soon as Chas's car had roared off towards Cheetham Green, the pretence of civility vanished.

'I thought I'd made myself plain when it came to your relationship with Chas! I suppose he forgot to tell you he's engaged to another woman?'

Cat presumed Chas's urgency to get home had something to do with romantic attachment. There was no reason why he should discuss it with her.

'Chas merely wanted to explain why he negotiated the contract the way he did. It was no more than that. Anyway——' she tossed back her ebony curls '—I don't have to account to you for my movements outside working hours. I can see who I like.'

She heard his indrawn breath, sensing the impatience in him. 'He's engaged to Serena Hamilton. Her father owns the Hamilton Group of hotels. Do you honestly believe that Chas will turn his back on all that? Looking at the mess he's made of this deal, he has no choice but to marry well. I can't see his silk suits faring well mucking out horses.'

Steve's voice was hard and uncompromising. If she

had cherished dreams in that direction, she would have been devastated.

'Don't worry,' she reassured him with syrupy sincerity. 'I wouldn't dream of getting in the way of your empire-building. Chas is quite safe from me.'

Steve laughed derisively. 'I really don't get it. If someone had cheated me the way Chas cheated you, I wouldn't give him the time of day. Why do worthless men appeal to women so much? Maybe you could tell me.'

'I'm sure you're not short of theories,' she responded smartly. 'You consider yourself an authority on most things.'

'Not on women. They never cease to baffle me.'

Cat rather doubted that. He could make her blood-pressure rise with very little effort. 'We prefer puppies to wolves, Mr Lucas. They're easier to handle.'

'I haven't bitten you yet. Chas has. What makes him less threatening?'

'Because he's thoughtless rather than dangerous. You would go for the jugular.'

'Yes,' he agreed softly, his breath warm against her skin as the path brought them close together. 'I would. So why do you keep baring your pretty white neck?'

His words made her stumble, the sudden grip of his hand on her arm a support and a threat at the same time. Cold sweat laced her spine.

'We're not likely to be friends, are we?' Her voice sounded off-centre. 'It was cruel making me bring about the end of Farrells. Why did you do that?' She wilfully changed the subject, bringing them back to familiar territory.

'Would it have been easier for you to sit back and let me do it?' The heavy irony in his voice suggested he knew the answer to that. 'Besides, running a business is not all good times. Ranleigh needs dragging into the real world and so, beautiful, do you.'

Cat began to see what Chas was up against. Steve Lucas's brand of people management was based on the arrogant view that he knew what was best for them. If he thought she was going to be grateful for being introduced to the destructive world of property development then he was sadly mistaken.

'The past can teach us a lot,' she retorted, fire in her veins. 'About community and caring. You're going to replace a living estate with transient visitors who are trying to escape exactly what your sort have created.'

Steve stopped and turned her around to face him, the moon high in the sky, casting their faces in silver. 'You're talking to the wrong man. You should have pleaded your case to Edward Ranleigh. He had the power to maintain this museum. I have to serve my investors. Taking on an estate that at best would break even wouldn't interest them.'

Cat glared at him frustratedly. She had been surprised by the lack of provision made by Edward Ranleigh but she could excuse that, knowing how devastated the old man had been by his son's death.

'Don't pretend you're not enjoying this,' she hurled at him. 'I've seen you walking the course, gloating over your achievement.'

'I like to see things taking shape,' he agreed. 'I think you'll find the other tenants who have moved out aren't as unhappy with their lot as you are.' His tone was reasonable but the tension between them was building.

'As if you care!' Cat gasped. 'I suppose you've asked them, have you? Or do you just take it upon yourself to know what's best for people?'

'That sounds like one of Chas's lines,' he observed critically. 'You seem addicted to lost causes.'

Cat visibly controlled her temper, shaking with the effort, her dark eyes pools of fury. 'I promise you, I'm not addicted to Chas. This public haunting can stop.'

'Public haunting? Sorry, I'm lost.'

'Oh!' Her enraged cry bore witness to her exasperation with the man. 'You're everywhere I turn,' she accused him, escaping his dominating presence by taking up the pace once more, aware of him falling into step beside her.

'You think I followed you to the Swan?' His feigned surprise was mockery incarnate.

'I suppose I imagined your attitude tonight. Catherine will do this, Catherine won't do that. I'm sure Penelope Cheetham will be spreading far and wide what her idea of a "personal assistant" is!'

Steve Lucas blocked her path, his longer strides easily outpacing her, his hand grasping a low hanging branch of a tree. He was smiling, she could hear it in his voice.

'You're upset because I don't want you to split your head open on an unsuitable horse.'

'I'm upset——' she spoke between her teeth '—because you presume the right to make decisions for me!'

Ducking under his arm, she put up hand to protect her hair from small outlying branches, hearing him follow her at a leisurely pace.

'I thought you were in favour of paternalistic employers, Catherine. Why should my concern bother you so much?'

'There's nothing paternalistic about it. For some twisted reason of your own, you want people to think we're involved. Perhaps it's ego or a desire to tarnish me in Chas's eyes——'

'Maybe it's wishful thinking,' Steve provided, sounding amused. 'I find you attractive, it's as simple as that.'

'I doubt that.' Cat hugged her thin jacket to her body, her heart beating madly. Ranleigh was clearly visible, so too the cottages clustered around the estate path, some of the windows still lit.

'What? That I find you attractive?' He was charming her and she resisted the temptation he offered.

'That there's anything simple about your motives,' she ventured crossly. Pausing as they approached the stable path, she prepared to dismiss him. 'I'll check the stables before I go to bed. There's no need for you to accompany me.'

'Security cover the stables as well as the rest of the estate. If anything's wrong, they'll let you know.'

'They know about horses, do they?' she asked sweetly. 'There's a grey called Flossie that I think may be coming down with something. I can hardly move her to another stable if she's contagious. I thought you'd applaud my diligence.'

Glancing at his watch, Steve waved her forward, following her despite her obvious abhorrence of his company.

'You don't need to come,' she repeated, digging in her pockets for the keys to the tack-room, aware of his tall broadly built figure shadowing her movements.

'Call it old-fashioned chivalry. I don't think young ladies should be alone in the dark.' His tone made it clear that he wasn't talking about anything chivalrous at all.

Ignoring him, she picked up one of the battery-powered lanterns. He watched her determined figure, following her to the stable, moving to help her with the stiff latch, watching as the grey mare's head became visible.

'She's sweating up,' Cat murmured almost to herself, patting the horse's neck. 'I think it might be colic. I'll have to ring the vet.'

'I'm expecting a call in half an hour. How long will you be?'

'I'll have to wait,' she explained patiently. 'I can't leave a sick horse. There's a camp bed in the tack-room. Don't worry, I've done this hundreds of times, I really don't need a watchdog.'

'You're staying out here alone? Are you crazy?' Steve Lucas caught her as she would have moved past him. 'I'll get one of the security guards over until I can get back.'

She was about to argue with him but she could see that he was determined. Shrugging carelessly, she watched him take a portable phone out of his jacket and arrange a baby-sitter. She was putting the horse blanket on Flossie when the guard arrived and nodded briefly at the man, instructing him to sit in the tack-room. 'There's no need for both of us to get cold,' she commented.

'Here.' Steve took off his jacket. Silently she took it from him, taking his Filofax out of the pocket and handing it back.

'Thanks.' His tone was dry, aware of the unspoken significance. Cat didn't want to be accused of poaching his secrets. She was well aware of his mistrust.

Watching him go, Cat was aware of certain misgivings. His warmth clung to the jacket and surrounded her. Steve Lucas was an unpredictable man, his masculine views on protecting the fairer sex surprising her and bringing back vague memories of the past. Used to being independent, she didn't want Steve Lucas exposing any weakness, finding chinks in her armour.

By the time Steve returned, she was sure her diagnosis was correct. It was important to keep a horse warm and moving if it had colic, otherwise it might injure itself or go down in the stable.

Protected by a thick leather jacket, he took the reins from her cold fingers. 'There's a Thermos in the tack-room. Pour yourself some coffee.'

For once she didn't argue with him. She was cold and a hot drink sounded wonderful.

The vet came at half-past three in the morning, confirming Cat's suspicions and congratulating her on her first aid.

'I don't suppose we can go to bed now?' Steve queried without much hope.

'You can go to bed any time you like,' Cat returned but without any real fire. 'Flossie should be all right now but I'll stay until the stable lads arrive.'

'You don't have to do this to impress me,' he growled. 'You're supposed to be in my office in less than four hours.'

'I'll be there, don't worry.' Her chin lifted proudly, dark eyes shining with challenge.

'I'm sure you will,' he returned with equal steel. 'Well, you can martyr yourself if you like.' He sized up the camp bed and sat down on it gingerly, testing its weight. 'We'll go to Ranleigh for breakfast. Wake me up if anything exciting happens. Or wake me up if you want something exciting to happen.' He grinned at her haughty expression.

'Don't hold your breath,' she muttered, turning on her heel and hearing his soft laughter follow her out into the dark stable yard.

Cat checked the grey mare, relieved to find her more contented, and returned to the tack-room. The lantern illuminated Steve's hunched figure on the camp bed. His skin took on the colour of tarnished gold in the dim light, the growth of stubble roughening his jaw emphasising his masculine nature.

Why had he stayed? It would have been enough to have ensured one of his security men spent the night watching over her. He surely couldn't believe she had planned a further rendezvous with Chas! She smiled at the idea. If he did, he would have an uncomfortable night to reward his suspicions.

After checking Flossie for the second time, Cat made herself a cup of coffee, the smell rich on the air.

'That smells good.' The sleep-thickened voice made her jump. Steve propped himself up on one elbow, saying 'thanks' when she made him a cup. Cat sat down on one of the scarred chairs with her own mug warming her hands.

'Doesn't anyone worry when you disappear in the middle of the night?' Steve regarded her through the steam from his coffee, taking a mouthful and wincing. 'Smells better than it tastes.'

'It's instant. The Thermos is empty.' She knew he preferred filtered coffee. 'I'm always out early in the morning. My mother goes to bed just after ten. She's a heavy sleeper and she trusts me. . . Why, do you think I should be under lock and key?'

Steve Lucas took in the youthful independence she projected with a cynical twist to his mouth. 'Something like that. What happens if you meet up with some madman in the middle of the night? What would you do then?'

Cat blinked as if the thought had never occurred to her. 'We're rather out of the way at Ranleigh,' she demurred, sipping her coffee.

'Out of the way!' He put down the barely touched coffee. 'You're in a time warp, babe.'

'No,' she replied her voice thickening. 'I'm in what's

left of rural England. When I was growing up we didn't
need fences or security men to keep Ranleigh safe. The
estate workers looked after each other.'

'And threw out undesirables.' He met her gaze, his
own heavy with the undertow of memory.

'If they needed to.' Cat's eyes narrowed in concentration. 'Why do you resent Ranleigh's past so much?
Is it something to do with your mother? I've never
heard anything——'

'Bad about her?' Steve finished the sentence. 'If
she'd stayed on the estate, we might have been neigh-
bours. Maybe shared your first kiss.' His mouth turned
up at the corners at her sudden flare of colour.

'But then you wouldn't have been you,' she pointed
out to cover up her embarrassment. 'The American
half would be missing.'

'The accent, maybe.' Lying back, he put his hands
behind his head, staring at the ceiling. 'My mother
used to tell me stories about this place. It sounded like
heaven compared to the fleapits we stayed in. I used to
think about stowing away on a boat and. . .' He sighed
as if he was tired with himself. 'And now I'm here,
telling stories to a little girl who should know better
than to spend a night with a strange man in a stable.'

'He won't go away. What can I do?' she appealed,
feeling drawn in by his memories and wanting to know
more. 'Is that why you wanted to develop the estate?
Because it was something you couldn't have when you
were young?'

'Not at all.' Closing his eyes, he shut her out. 'Are
you going to talk all night? I like women who know
when to sleep.'

Cat regarded him with a frown. End of the conversation, she realised. There was something about the
way Steve Lucas talked about Ranleigh that didn't add

up. If it had been the focus of some childhood dream, why was he so determined to change it? She tried to recall his exact words and found his voice murmuring through her mind as she dozed, huddled in his jacket.

Her head nodded, consciousness returning and drifting away again. Something obligingly solid cushioned her head and a pleasant haze of heat surounded her. She breathed in a spicy scent, her nose twitching, trying to capture it.

Dawn came soft and gentle, the dew glistening on the grass in the nearby paddock. Cat awoke to view sleepily the sight of a rabbit, ears pricked for sound. The sun hung low in the sky, a golden blur, promising a warm, hazy day to crown the golden harvest of high summer.

'Beautiful, isn't it?' A voice near her ear purred into her consciousness and for a moment seemed as natural as the bright chatter of birds and the fresh beauty of a new morning.

Jumping to her feet, she took in her vacant chair to see another alongside it, occupied by her tormentor of the evening before.

Steve Lucas viewed her consternation with a gleam of humour. 'We were both cold; it seemed practical.'

She had slept in his arms! The knowledge disturbed her intensely. Cat didn't have time to tell him what she thought about his liberty-taking. Jamie and the two stable lads arrived, allowing her to relieve her feelings in a blistering attack on their laxity.

'Who let Flossie drink cold water after a long run? Do you know how much pain she was in? She was biting her sides.'

Jamie looked shame-faced. 'I didn't realise she'd been out,' he admitted. 'You know I don't know anything about horses. I did my best.'

'Seems as if you should try a little harder.' Steve lounged in the tack-room door, looking sleepy. 'If you do it again, you'll spend the night walking round the stable yard, while your sister and I have a little more comfort.'

Cat froze as three pairs of eyes fixed on the American. It was obvious that he had spent the night there with her. He looked rumpled, a dark growth of beard shadowing his jaw, but still managing to look infinitely sexy to Cat's sore eyes.

'I'll deal with this.' She tried to claw back her authority.

'Yes, boss,' he mocked her softly, but waited for her while she issued a series of orders as to the management of the stables.

'You've done it again,' she muttered when they were out of hearing of the others.

'Done what?' He fingered his jaw, the short stubble rasping against his skin, blue eyes lazy with invitation as they returned her indignant gaze.

'That line about us having more comfort. You make it sound as if we're——'

'Sleeping together,' he offered with a tilting of his lips, fighting not to smile.

'Yes!'

'Sorry, I didn't think. We'll spend the day on the boat,' he informed her as they walked wearily back towards Ranleigh.

'The boat?' Her dazed mind was non-comprehending.

'At Markham. You can catch up on your sleep while the crew put her through her paces, then I'll need you to take notes.'

'You could use a dictaphone,' she retorted peevishly. 'I'd be more use here.'

'I don't want you here. And I'm your boss,' he underlined in case she had forgotten the fact.

'Whatever you say, sir.' She was painfully polite.

'You're getting the idea.'

They were back on familiar territory, griping at each other, and Cat felt a little easier.

'Am I allowed to get changed?' she queried innocently. 'It will mean leaving your side for all of half an hour.'

'I think I can manage without you for that long. Although, if it makes you feel insecure, I'm quite willing to watch.'

She winced a smile and headed off towards the cottage, feeling as if she had been given a temporary reprieve from her gaoler.

'I'll order your breakfast,' he called after her.

She shivered, and it wasn't with cold. Steve Lucas was entwining himself around her like a quick-growing vine. She had spent over twenty-four hours in his company with no reprieve. No doubt he was making sure that she had little opportunity to meet Chas, so she couldn't spike the family's merger with the Hamiltons.

Chas presented little threat to her peace of mind. It was Steve whose image was imprinted on every cell of her body! While she showered and put on fresh clothes, she felt lacking in the vital energy his close proximity engendered. It was this insidious attraction that worried her. She didn't even like him and yet she was aware of deep emotion stirring within her that she seemed powerless to control.

Dressing in black denims and a mustard-coloured sweatshirt, she pulled on a waterproof jacket and descended the stairs, leaving a note for her mother telling her she had gone to Markham.

Steve was eating a full English breakfast when she arrrived, and invited her to follow his example. She declined and nibbled on a slice of toast.

'Lost your appetite?' He surveyed her figure at his leisure. 'It can't be the calories—all that horse-riding must burn them up.'

She bit into the toast, her neat white teeth a little more savage than normal when addressing her breakfast.

'Girls and horses. Do you think it's a subliminal desire for power? Controlling brute strength?'

'Men ride too,' she pointed out coolly. 'It's a lot of fun. I wouldn't look any deeper than that.'

'No,' he agreed, 'you wouldn't. I think you're too tied up with being head girl at home to consider your own needs very much.'

'This is when I'm not seducing your executives, is it?' Her smile was glassy.

'I'm holding judgement on that. I can't imagine you seducing anyone.' Smoky blue eyes surveyed her rigid figure, perched on a chair. 'Whoever nicknamed you Cat made a mistake. You're more like a kitten: all sharp teeth and claws, no strategy at all.'

Cat digested his words, watching him finish his coffee and rise to his feet. Determinedly chewing her toast, she stubbornly refused to be rushed. She didn't know what he meant by 'strategy'. Her aims were simple and he knew them. He made it sound as though she was an amateur, trying to execute a sophisticated plan and failing hopelessly.

'Coming?' Steve regarded her with a quirked eye-brow, watching her take a sip of tea without any apparent hurry.

'Yes, I've finished now, thank you,' she pertly under-lined his lack of manners.

Hooking his fingers under the collar of his white and black Helly Hansen jacket, he waved her to precede him out of the room.

'After you, princess.'

Her gaze swept over him in regal condescension. Getting up, she stalked past him, only to squeak with outrage when he smartly smacked her backside.

'How dare you?' she spluttered, as he took her arm and urged her forward with a piratical grin.

'That's the problem with playing lady of the manor. There's always some rough type who forgets to bow and scrape.'

'Well, that certainly describes you,' she fumed, seeing his grin widen, hurrying on in front of him so that he didn't get the chance to repeat the chastisement.

CHAPTER FIVE

CAT'S eyes felt sore and gritty as they travelled to Markham. She was determined not to fall asleep again. The last time they were on the *Seagull*—was it really only two days ago?—they'd had a blazing row.

She resented being dragged along on what she considered a purely recreational trip, and her mutinous expression was an open book.

Sea-blue eyes swept critically across her features, Steve's mouth hardening as he negotiated the Range Rover around a sharp bend.

'I'll remember you're a woman that needs her sleep. For future reference, few employers enjoy a sour-faced, sharp-tongued shrew in their employment—it's bad PR.'

'I have things to do!' she fretted. 'Paperwork—bills to pay, receipts to issue. I know all you think Farrells needs is a bulldozer but——'

'No buts. Farrells is history. The future begins here. Get used to it!'

It was a cruel, brutal reminder and his profile was ungiving. A shocked quiver ran through Cat. She felt he was punishing her for something more than being a loose end he had to tie up. It was there again, the same sensation of grievance. Was it the comfortable security of her past that grated on him or was it something more personal?

By the time they reached Markham, Cat had resolved to mask her feelings and hide how much his callous disposal of her lifestyle hurt her.

She viewed the boat doubtfully when the Range
Rover drew up at the marina. Its hull was resplendent
with a coat of black enamel, the smell of varnish strong
as they approached.

'Is it ready to sail?' she asked dubiously, hoping
there would be some last-minute hitch. Cat hadn't
much experience of seaworthy yachts and this elderly
conversion, although sturdy to look at, made her feel a
little apprehensive.

'We'll soon find out.' Steve Lucas eyed her with
heartless determination. 'Does your bravery only
extend to horses?'

'I know about horses,' she pointed out.

'Well, I know about sailing,' he offered in return.
'Get on board.'

'Aye, aye, Captain Bligh,' she muttered under her
breath, gingerly clambering on to the boat.

Steve didn't have much time for her after that. He
was involved in discussions with Jack and Pete, the
other two crew members, instructing her to find a bunk
and catch up on her sleep. Cat gave him a killing look,
knowing what the others had made of that.

Wearily, she stayed on deck until the yacht had
gained the open sea. The promise of a warm summer's
day had evaporated into overcast skies and a keen sea
breeze. The wind was cold and her lack of sleep made
her feel it keenly. For a moment she let herself dwell
on that fraction of time when she had awoken to the
magic of a new day in the warm strength of Steve
Lucas's arms. Watching him stride the deck, shouting
instructions, she found it hard to imagine that brief,
fleeting harmony. He was a man of action, not sensi-
tivity, and if for a moment they had been in tune, it
had probably been calculated to seek some advantage
over her.

'You'd better go below,' Jack advised, his face weatherbeaten into a permanent ruddy brown. 'There's a cold wind. It'll cut you in two if you stay up here.'

Steve's head turned, his eyes as hospitable as the sea, a mocking smile acknowledging her as a spare part in this arduous pursuit.

Deciding that getting cold and miserable on deck was going to prove very little, apart from her own stupidity, she descended below.

Cat counted her blessings. She didn't suffer from sea-sickness and found the motion of the boat surging through the waves as conducive to sleep as a baby being rocked in a crib.

Slipping in and out of dreams, Cat was dimly aware of the sound of the wind. She heard Steve's voice several times but he seemed calm, his voice holding elements of the satisfaction that came from a challenge well met. When he wasn't being vile, he was a very capable man, she thought sleepily.

Wafts of warm food woke her up, her stomach protesting and her nose twitching. Eyes fraying apart, Cat had the feeling that she had slept for some time.

As she scrambled off the bunk, the sleeping bag slipped from under her, speeding her descent, and she fell with a thump to the floor. The varnished boards offered nothing to break her fall and dark startled eyes lifted to see a pair of deck shoes and denim-clad legs.

'Decided to show a little respect at last.' A hateful, all too familiar, voice drawled.

Cat was unceremoniously hoisted to her feet by one strong hand. The other, she saw, was supporting a pizza. She'd had no more than a slice of toast all day and her mouth watered.

'Do you want some of this?' He placed the box in the galley. 'I don't like eating on my own'.

Cat frowned non-comprehendingly. 'Are we back at Markham? I'm sorry. I seem to have slept through the entire voyage. You should have woken me up.'

Steve shrugged, his eyes watchful as if expecting a different reaction. 'You can make up the work tomorrow. We'll be out longer than I expected.'

'What?' Cat frowned. 'I thought we were in harbour, the boat——'

'We are,' he cut in. 'But not Markham. We've taken shelter at Cowes—the Isle of Wight. We'll make the return journey tomorrow.'

'The Isle of Wight?' Cat squeaked. 'I don't understand!'

'It's quite simple. Force four turned to Force seven and it's building. It seemed a good idea to wait for the storm to blow itself out. It's all right, I've told Jessica we won't be back until tomorrow.'

'You. . . When? How could you?'

'I called from the yacht club. We can go there later if you like.'

'I don't want to go to the yacht club!' She almost spelt out each word. 'I want to be home, not in the middle of the damn sea with you.'

'We're in harbour,' he explained, as if she were an idiot.

'Don't split hairs!'

The smile in his eyes burrowed under her skin. Cat's gaze was blurred by a red mist.

'You're pleased about this, aren't you? Why? What crooked scheme have you cooked up? Are my family being evicted while I'm imprisoned on this boat with you?'

'Scheme?' His lips depressed at her florid exaggeration. 'Working for me isn't nine-to-five. You've got a new job, honey. Forget your provincial little ideas and get into shape. Tomorrow it could be New York.'

'New York! You can't just hire someone to keep you company. I don't actually do anything useful, apart from provide you with some sort of warped revenge.'

'You could help me crew the yacht. It's an investment the same as any other. Excuse me for thinking you'd had a hard night and might need some rest.'

She was momentarily stunned, but not out of any feeling of remorse.

'You're going to sell this? The yacht?'

'Sure. Why not? I might keep it and run it as a charter,' he amended thoughtfully.

Cat couldn't understand him. She might not be enamoured with life on the high seas, but she knew by his pride when showing her the boat and the sound in his voice when he captained her that he loved every gleaming inch of the *Seagull*.

'Why do you bother? Don't you value things of beauty? Doesn't anything have meaning for you?'

Steve Lucas merely shrugged. 'Craftsmen rarely keep what they make, Catherine. You can love something without owning it. I thought your experience at Ranleigh would have taught you that. Few of us have the luxury of possession. Time has a strange way of distorting things.'

She didn't understand what he meant about things being distorted, but the rest of it made her feel curious. Steve Lucas travelled light. He was a top-flight executive who played with boats in his spare time. He didn't have much time for other commitments. She wondered if he regarded women in the same superficial manner he did his other pastimes.

'Isn't there anything you would keep? Anything you'd consider painful to lose?'

'I wouldn't like to lose you.' He spoke with lazy seduction in his voice, his gaze resting on her sleep-flushed cheeks and vulnerable lips.

'You haven't got me to lose,' she denied heatedly, pushing a hand through her tangled locks, aware of his desire to avoid the subject by inflaming her temper.

'My most valued employee.' Steve laughed on a low growl of derision. 'Nothing's permanent, Catherine, but change itself.' He was laughing at her, tying her up in philosophical conundrums.

'Pretty words to hide the fact that you have no soul.'

'That's no way to speak to your employer,' he pointed out in a warning tone.

'Kidnapping people counts high in business etiquette, does it?'

Steve Lucas's jaw tightened with irritation. 'You can leave the boat any time you like, lady. You also have the privilege of resignation if the job doesn't suit you. Is that perfectly clear?'

Cat was stunned into silence. So that was his game. He was after her resignation!

'Very clear,' she applauded, broken glass in her voice.

'Good.' He was distracted for a moment by the hesitant tap on the door of the cabin.

'We're off now, Skip. See you later.'

'Yes, OK. Have a good time.' His voice warmed fractionally but the irritation was still there. Steve Lucas was not used to being thwarted. She guessed it was a long time since someone had ever dared regard him with the contempt she was blasting at him.

'In the morning you can get in supplies of food. Enough for lunch and some emergency supplies—tinned stuff.'

Cat didn't like the sound of an emergency. She

wouldn't be surprised if tomorrow he announced they were to cross the Atlantic.

'You might have told me there was a possibility of being held up. I haven't got anything to wear,' she muttered in a subdued tone. 'I haven't even got a toothbrush or nightclothes or anything.'

'Women,' Steve grunted, disappearing for a moment and coming back with a large T-shirt. 'Toiletries of a basic nature you'll find in the shower compartment. Anything else?'

Cat could think of a million things but in his present mood, she considered discretion the better part of valour. She wouldn't be obstructive but she damn well wasn't going to co-operate.

Steve busied himself in the small galley. Cutting the pizza, he put it on to two plates, scooping up a handful of cutlery and plonking the lot on to the table. He caught her critical regard and winced a smile.

'So I've never waited tables. You can tidy things up while I get the wine. Maybe we can drink this bottle.'

She was glad he had turned away. The memory of their argument aboard the *Seagull* brought back a rush of unease. He had a temper to match her own and Jack and Pete weren't on hand to calm the situation.

'Relax. I'd rather eat the pizza than take a bite out of you.'

Blushing bright red, Cat hated him for guessing what she was thinking so accurately. Determined not to let him put her off her share of the meal, she bit into a piece of pizza, eyeing him warily as he poured her a glass of red wine.

'I thought you disapproved of my drinking.' She couldn't resist the gibe.

'You're less appealing stone-cold sober,' he taunted in return. 'Besides, I warned you off that brew in the

Chalfont Cup because several of your male competitors
were trying to get their own back. Successful women
are a target for immature men. I didn't want to see
your pride trampled into the dust.' As he clipped her
glass lightly with his, a smile played around his mouth.
'Your fall from grace won't become a boy's-room story
because of me.'

Cat nearly choked. He could twist anything! 'A brief
kiss can hardly be counted as a fall from grace. Besides,
I wasn't drunk. I was a little merry, that's all. I knew
what I was. . .'

Cat came to an abrupt halt, prickles of tension
speeding up her spinal column. His eyes widened
questioningly, that mocking comprehension goading
her beyond endurance.

'You knew what you were doing.' He finished the
sentence. 'Are you saying you're a practised—let's be
kind and say flirt, with the ability to summon up
outraged innocence when your victim takes the bait?'

'No!'

'No?'

'No, I'm a normal female who can fall prey to
physical attraction when she's. . .'

'Merry?' he supplied aggravatingly.

'I didn't know how horrible you were then,' she
retorted childishly.

'I'm not horrible at all. I've saved your bacon more
than once. Besides, you weren't—er—merry the next
morning. It was more than a brief kiss then.'

Cat's dark eyes narrowed, shining like polished jet.
The conversation was getting alarmingly out of hand.

'Do you deny you're trying to hound me out of my
job?'

'Yes, I deny it.' The formal words were confounded
by the sensual meltdown playing havoc with her pros-

ecuting stance. How a mouth could seem to threaten when in reality it beckoned, how a blue gaze could consider her in that lazy reflective way and shred her defensive anger, she failed to fathom. But she found the progress of a piece of pizza to that sexy mouth managed to destroy her thought processes, and when he spoke she was suffering from a five-second delay in interpretation.

'However, to be fair, I have to tell you that in joining my workforce as a PA you have changed the nature of your work—comes under customs and practice in this country, I believe. If you quit the job, you quit Lucas-Brett for good. Goodbye, stables.' He made a farewell salute with an economy that redefined mockery.

'You——!'

Placing a hand firmly over her mouth, he leaned forward, his face separated from hers by a matter of inches. She could see the darker blue ring around his iris, the lashes spiking against his tanned skin. The warmth of his palm against her mouth sensitised her lips, and Cat fought the temptation to taste his flesh.

'I'm telling you this because I have a feeling you might get sacked for calling your employer insulting names.' Removing his hand, he saw that this time there was no delay in her response.

'You're laughing at me,' she accused, her eyes mirroring a mixture of emotions. 'If you mean to fire me, you might as well get it over with and save us both unpleasantness.'

Steve Lucas sighed, leaning back against the side of the bunk, taking a mouthful of red wine, a hint of exasperation firming his mouth.

'If I hired some no-hope kid off the street, she'd fall over herself to make a good impression. What I've got is a thorn in my side. If I didn't think you'd got a great pair of legs and the face of a gypsy queen, you'd be picking up a welfare cheque.'

Cat felt her heart somersault and caught her breath at his sheer nerve. Put at its most basic, he was saying she'd be out of a job if he didn't find her attractive.

'That's sexual harassment! What do you mean, no-hoper!' The words tumbled out and he had to check a smile.

'If anyone's been sexually harassed, it's me. And if you can't take the answer, don't ask me what I mean.'

Cat quivered visibly. The *Seagull* suddenly seemed very small, the space between them sizzling with intimacy.

'Can we forget Ranleigh for a few hours?' Steve invited, his tone gentling to a hynotic purr. 'I'm sick of playing the bad guy.'

Cat found the usual quick-fire response deserted her. 'I don't see how we can,' she mumbled, vigorously taking a bite of her rapidly cooling pizza to find her throat suddenly dry as he watched her lick the crumbs from her lips.

'Stop it,' she croaked, picking up her wine glass and taking a gulp.

'Stop what?'

He didn't get a response because the wine went down the wrong way, she coughed and managed to splash a generous measure down her front.

'Expensive wine should be tasted, not bolted down like bad medicine.' Steve took the glass from her hand and watched as she got up, exclaiming over the stain that she knew for certain had gone through to the lacy bra beneath.

With a flustered glance in his direction, she retrieved the T-shirt he had given her and went through to the shower cubicle, bright spots of colour marking both cheeks.

Discarding her sweatshirt and bra, she rinsed the red wine out of the material and pulled his T-shirt over her head, the soft cotton cascading over her, the shoulders halfway down her arms.

Her breasts budded against the masculine garment, and her eyes were hectic whirlpools of feeling. She couldn't avoid him. If she locked the door and stayed within the satefy of the cubicle, her humiliation would be complete. Pulling the cotton away from her skin, she had the brief assurance of shapelessness before her fingers released the catch, a deep shuddering breath gulped in an attempt to calm her jumping nerves.

Going back into the saloon took a lot of courage. Enduring the burning heat of his gaze over her trembling body was an exquisite torture.

'Are you all right?' He stood up, the communication between them unspoken but a powerful undertow, their eyes meeting in a bond of intimacy. His heavily fringed gaze magnified the sensuality of his expression. 'Why do I make you nervous?'

'You know why.' She tried to inch away from him but found he was in her path.

'Because when I kiss you you can't hate me,' he supplied, his voice becoming intimate and husky, wrapping her brain in cotton wool.

'I don't hate you exactly,' she stumbled, trying to get back to safe territory.

'I told you it was more complicated than hate.' He didn't sound as if he was concentrating on what he was saying and, when she lifted her gaze, she found he was looking at her mouth with raw demand.

'Steve. . .' Excitement washed through her body with all the force of a commando raid.

'Strictly off duty,' he muttered, his lashes lifting to open her to a potent assault. 'Let's find a little harmony, angel, before you drive me crazy.'

From a long way off, some sensible remnant of her sanity was saying, You shouldn't be doing this. . . But her lips parted, the soft inner silk a barely visible invitation. He drew her into his arms, warm, masculine lips descending slowly, a flash of blue fire searing her face as Steve Lucas read the need she hadn't a hope of disguising.

Resistance was as instinctive as the surge of response. Her neck arched back, the ebony river of her hair a running wave over her shoulders, her lips flinching away from his as if they scalded rather than caressed.

'You were eager enough last night.' His mouth slid over hers, biting at the trembling, velvet softness, his tongue licking the slight parting, sliding hotly across her jaw. 'All those sleepy, begging kisses.' His breath was hot against her skin, competing with the internal fireworks triggering Cat's responses.

'I did nothing of the sort.' Her outrage was barely a whisper. She closed her eyes as he pressed kisses over her cheekbones and eyelids, moving on to explore her forehead and the sculpted delicacy of her temples. 'You're making it up.'

His low growl of laughter against the sensitive hollow of her ear made her quiver noticeably and he pulled her closer, his hands sliding under the T-shirt he had lent her, travelling in a wave of fire over her back.

'Does it feel as if I'm making it up?' Steve's eyes had darkened to navy, his mouth heavy with sensuality as he gathered up the folds of cotton and slid the material up over her ribcage. Cat's breath shook in her throat, her fevered half-protest barely convincing.

Steve's mouth collided with hers, demanding an end to the ritualistic retreats of courtship. He swallowed the small murmurs of protest, lean fingers gliding over the curve of her breast and closing over it possessively.

'Now I know why I put up with all the noise.' He spoke against her mouth, his voice deep and intimate. 'You're like silk to touch. I want to stroke every inch of you. . .' His thumb worked against her nipple, his tongue making hot, indecent demands in her mouth. Cat shuddered under the force of such sensual pleasure, arching against the hard demand of his body. His hips welcomed her softness, his legs parting to accommodate her, imprisoning one slim thigh between his, easing the ache in his loins against her. Cat's inarticulate whisper was for more rather than less of this crude communication of need. When he broke from her mouth, her lips quivered with the loss.

'Let's forget the kids' stuff,' he muttered. 'We both want the same thing.'

'Steve. . .' Weakly her head rested back against the panelling, her cheeks hot, her eyes closing as she saw the intent in his gaze. It was impossible to tell him how little she knew, when she was so very eager to learn.

Holding a fistful of material in one hand near her left shoulder, he bared her breasts, his eyes electric as he urged one small nipple to full ripeness.

It was an exquisite torture to let him prepare her for his pleasure, but to deny the insistent nag of her own desires was beyond her. 'I want to know if you taste as delicious as you look. . .' His words drifted into her mind. She had wanted this then, on their first meeting. Her fingers threaded into his dark hair, moulding his powerful skull, unable to satiate the hungering burn in her body.

Pressing hard kisses over her upper chest and throat,

his groan of impatience shivered over her skin. 'You make me feel like a savage. I just want to rip everything off you and take you here. . .'

Cat wished he would! Her fingers ran lightly over his cheek, pressing against the hard bone, his mouth turning against her palm, before his gaze consumed hers with passionate demand.

'Kiss me. . .' His hands gripped her waist, pulling her closer, his head bending to tempt her into action.

The newness of the experience made her hesitate. His fingers tightened against her and she shadowed his mouth with her own, drawn to him, drawn to tempt and tease, feeling a feminine thrill at the impatience in his touch. Delicately licking the masculine contours of his mouth, she allowed herself the luxury of delving into the moist warmth, Steve in return communicating his own desire with raunchy simplicity. Feverishly, her hand burrowed under his jersey and caressed him with a shy eroticism that made his skin leap under her touch as if she had burnt him.

Cat was dazzled by his masculine beauty. His body heat tingled against her fingers, his musky masculine scent drifted to her nostrils and she nuzzled his throat, her mouth opening against his brown skin, white teeth kittenish in play, her tongue soothing the slight abrasions she made. She felt him still, his chest restricted as if it hurt to breathe.

'You're sure you want to live with biting me?' Steve's voice rumbled against her ear, his hand stroking the midnight darkness of her hair, enjoying the dark river of silk washing through his fingers.

Frowning, she tilted her head back to look up into his handsome features. A dark eyebrow quizzed her. Tracing the line of her jaw with his index finger, pausing at the corner of her sweet pink mouth, he watched her eyes take in the bruise she had made with growing horror.

He slowly and deliberately explored her throat, letting his fingers dip into the delicate hollow at its base. Blue eyes lifted from the perusal of her silky skin to challenge her.

'If you want to scratch and bite, I'll give you a reason.'

'No, please—don't.' She tried desperately to climb out of the dream she was in, but his mouth against her throat was overwhelmingly persuasive.

'Damn!' His oath was harsh and heartfelt. He raised his head as footsteps came clearly from the region of the deck. Cat blinked with realisation as he pulled the T-shirt down in a quick drag over her sensitised body.

'Oh. . .' Jack smiled benevolently. 'Don't let me interrupt, I'm off to bed. Family had company,' he offered as an excuse.

Cat, still in Steve's arms, stiffened, the passionate drowse in her eyes igniting into something less inviting.

'You planned this! That's why you decided on Cowes rather than the mainland. Of all the. . .'

She tried to push him away, emitting a squeal of outrage as she was flattened against his chest, her hair used as a rope to tether her as Steve Lucas wound it round his fist. Frustration and fury glittered in his eyes.

'If I'd planned it, we wouldn't be on a boat with bunk beds fit for midgets. And let's get things straight—you were kissing me, you were touching me, and wasn't it you that did this?'

Cat viewed the mark on his throat with undiluted shame. The indisputable evidence of complicity was there for all to see.

'Nothing terrible's going to happen if you admit you

want me,' Steve murmured coaxingly. 'I want you
too.'

'I'd rather sleep with a boa constrictor!' She glared
at him. 'Will you let me go!'

'Certainly.' He let her free as if she was something
contagious. 'I'll bunk in the captain's cabin. You can
stay in here and dream up reasons why you're not a
tease and why one gulp of wine severely prejudices
your virtue. Goodnight, Catherine.'

He secured the locks so that no one else could enter
the cabin and then left without another word. The
thumps coming from the captain's cabin suggested he
wasn't exactly pleased with the way the evening had
ended.

Cat was horrified at her own weakness. Tides of
excitement churned in her stomach, her skin goose-
pimpled hot and cold, her fevered senses picking up
every sound coming from the cabin he occupied.

The violence of her passion startled her. She wanted
to rampage in fury, melt into honeyed weakness, find
oblivion in his arms and never see him again all at the
same time.

Having to sleep in his T-shirt didn't help. Gritting
her teeth, she tried to ignore her own reaction. The
most seductive silk could not have disturbed her more.
Even when she managed to be rid of his presence, he
was still wrapped around her.

Sliding into the sleeping bag, she put out the small
light above her head and listened for the sound of his
breathing. Instead, she picked up the insistent rhythm
of the sea. It reminded her of the wind heaving and sigh-
ing in the copse at Ranleigh. Finding some comfort in
that, she let her eyelids droop, retreating into dreams
of the past, when life had seemed simple, the pattern of
the seasons bringing known and manageable problems.

She sighed, her dark lashes flickering, her fingers tracing the embroidered monogram on the shirt she wore.

There was to be no peace; he chased her through her dreams. . .

CHAPTER SIX

'DOES making love always make you so quiet? You'll make someone a wonderful wife.'

Cat was swamped with embarrassment, her dark eyes darting at Steve's profile, thankful he was concentrating on driving the Range Rover. How could she possibly work with him now?

She had occupied herself that morning in the small galley of the pilot cutter, avoiding Steve as much as the limitations of the boat allowed. It had been a nerve-racking journey coming back from Markham; only as they neared Ranleigh had she let herself relax a little.

'I don't see what you're getting so worked up about.' His voice was cool with mockery. 'We hardly got past first base.'

Cat sent him a speaking look. First base, indeed. It was further than she cared to go with him and it had left her feeling out of control and extremely vulnerable.

'You look tired.' His provocation continued, devilment in his eyes. 'I didn't sleep much either. I kept dreaming of this beautiful, dark-haired vampire trying to drink my blood——'

'Shut up!' She was mortified.

Steve smiled, his hand squeezing her knee, laughing with wicked male enjoyment as she slapped it away.

'I see. You're going to turn all prim and proper again, are you? Spend your time giving me prickly heat in the office.'

Cat swallowed drily, not trusting her voice. He insisted on thinking she was a tease. If only he knew the truth! He was the only male in her life who could send her hormones into over-drive, the only male who made her weak at the knees with a passing glance.

'Would you drop me off at the stables, please?' Cat was stiffly formal. It was a matter of survival to distance their relationship into something more professional. So far the boundaries had been wilfully blurred on Steve's part, allowing him to exploit the underlying sexual tension between them, transforming every encounter into one fraught with danger.

'I thought you were desperate for a shower and a change of clothes.' Steve's jawline hardened impatiently as he slowed down to obey her request, the Range Rover bumping over the uneven, sparsely gravelled track leading to Farrells.

'I just want to check everything's all right. You did say I could have what's left of the afternoon off,' she reminded him with an attempt at patience.

'So I did.' His voice echoed her attempt at civility, his teasing replaced by an air of sharp determination.

Bringing the Range Rover to a halt, Steve leant against the wheel, aware of Cat's flinch of shock and the hostile stiffening of her body. Viewing the gouged hole where a redundant shed had been, his mouth compressed, his light eyes flicking sideways in jaundiced expectation.

'Don't tell me. . . It was a listed building? A vital part of Ranleigh's heritage?'

Trembling with the effort of suppressing her feelings, Cat didn't respond. Her white face spoke for her and Steve Lucas viewed her with a mixture of exasperation and sympathy.

'If it helps, I knew nothing about this. But what difference does a couple of days make? It has to happen some time, Catherine. Why prolong the agony?'

Cat pushed open the door of the Range Rover, scrambled out and walked slowly to the square of naked earth. She blinked hard, wishing he'd leave her alone.

'I'm surprised you didn't man the bulldozer yourself,' she flung at him as he joined her. 'After all, no one deserves the honour of demolishing Farrells more!'

'Catherine. . .' His cautioning growl of her name brought the dark accusation of her eyes to his face. He actually had the gall to feel sorry for her! She pulled away as he reached for her, the appearance of one of the stable lads leading Shannon breaking into their private battle.

'Why don't you go?' she intoned with feeling. 'I'm sure you could manage to dictate a couple of eviction orders before tea. The day wouldn't be a total loss then, would it?'

'Not a bad idea,' he slung back at her. 'I may even add a termination of contract, really make it worthwhile.'

Cat didn't wait to listen. Moving towards Shannon, she muttered her intention to Johnnie before mounting the horse in one lithe movement.

Steve Lucas grabbed the bridle, detaining her, his gaze harsh and commanding. Cat's hand itched for a riding crop as livid anger etched itself on her features.

'Lose your temper on that horse. If you try it on me, you'll be in for a very rough ride!'

Cat felt her colour rise at the message in his eyes. She urged Shannon forward with a smart dig of her heels and was relieved when Steve moved back and she was released from his hateful presence. As it was, she couldn't relax until she heard the low hum of the ignition being fired and knew he wasn't watching her.

Tears glittered on her cheeks. She had never felt

more confused. Restless energy flowed through her veins. Escaping Steve wasn't much of a relief. It was as if she carried him with her. The alien rhythm of his voice, the way he moved, the overwhelming aura of masculinity he projected, replayed endlessly on her senses. He threatened everything she held dear, so why was that so hard to remember? Those sexy blue eyes only had to turn up the heat and every sensible thought in her head was demolished.

Stirring Shannon into a rousing gallop, Cat tried to lose herself in the sheer exhilaration of the ride. It took some time before she calmed herself enough to slow Shannon to a trot. Taking a deep gulp of air, she removed her hat, so that the wind could cool her scalp. Absently, she noted that the light was going and shadows were developing around her. Breathing in the earthy scent of grass and trees, she grasped at the fragile sense of peace and hugged it to her.

Riding around Ranleigh, she had first-hand experience of the changes taking place. The estate, she grudgingly admitted, was an ideal setting for the enterprise Lucas-Brett had in mind. A golf course, set in the grounds of a site of natural beauty, couldn't fail to make its mark on the traditional circuit.

Subtle changes were being engineered, the design pruning the natural scenery to fit in with the course requirements. The lightning-struck oak she had played on as a child had gone, so too several poplars removed from a line of elegant trees. It gave view to a glimpse of the lake, the dark water reflecting the sunset, moorhens and mallards visible as black dots on its surface.

'Walk on.' She needed a minimal movement of her heels against Shannon's sides before he obeyed.

The blast of a horn in the distance made her look

sharply back at the road leading to the manor house.
The Range Rover was bearing down on her, lights
flashing, clearly indicating she was wanted.

'Not on your life, buster!' She envisaged another
invasion of her time and with a swift kick of her heels
urged Shannon forward.

The bay, given its head, plunged into the trees,
weaving in and out of the small copse before coming
out into meadowland, jumping the beck and swinging
in a wide arc across the park. Leaning over Shannon's
neck, Cat caught sight of the Range Rover off the
road, following her across the most direct route possible. She should have left the park! The landscaping
necessary for the golf course had smoothed out some
of the quirks of the terrain and a Range Rover was
ideally suited for the sort of territory she was being
hunted across.

Dark eyes alive with the challenge, her black hair
flying around her face, she made that man-handled
machine make a fight of it. Using Shannon's show-
jumping prowess, she wheeled and turned, racing
across towards the lake, her mind fixing on a plan, a
gurgle of glee breaking from her lips.

Cat was astride her horse when the Range Rover
pulled up and Steve Lucas pushed the door open,
barely restrained anger pulsating from him in waves.
Coming to stand six feet away from the small island
she inhabited with the help of her clean-jumping steed,
he clapped his hands in mocking appreciation of her
efforts.

'I haven't followed you to play games, Catherine.
Come back over here.'

'Why should I? I like it fine where I am.'

For a moment the flare of challenge ignited between

them but Steve remembered his mission and the battle light died in his eyes to be replaced by serious concern.

'Catherine, your mother has been taken to hospital. She had a bad asthma attack while she was having tea with one of her friends. I told your brother I'd find you.'

'Oh, no.' Her horrified expression softened his anger.

'I'll drive you to the hospital. I'm sure she'll be all right.'

Cat urged Shannon back across the shallow ford and slid down off the horse's back. 'He'll find his way back to the stables but I'll have to find someone to take care of him.'

'You can phone the house from the car. Get in, before I give in to my worst instincts and put you over my knee.'

Cat obeyed, totally subdued. She'd led him quite a dance and he'd only been trying to help her family out. Deep in shame, she tried to frame an apology.

'What were you running from? I don't usually chase my employees over hill and dale without a good reason.'

'I'm sorry.' Her face white, her mouth shaking with strain, she couldn't respond to his sarcasm. Her mother hadn't had a serious attack for over two years, although they had been frequent after George Farrell's death. She could only think the recent uncertainty over their future at Ranleigh had brought this one on.

'I'm sorry you felt you had to run,' he muttered under his breath, but she heard it and for a moment regarded his profile non-comprehendingly.

Flashing her an assessing glance, he leant over and fastened her seatbelt, taking the car phone out of its station and making it ready for use. She pushed the buttons necessary while he fired up the engine.

'Hold on,' he instructed, the low-impact warning muted in accusation. It was her fault they were in for a bumpy ride and she knew it. After gasping a few pertinent instructions to Johnnie, she replaced the phone and hung on for dear life. Steve clearly wasn't in the mood to take any prisoners as they ploughed through the intervening grassland back towards the estate.

Jessica Farrell was in a private room with an oxygen mask on, the familiar nebuliser bubbling away as it eased the condition of her constricted airway. It was a disturbing sight to those not used to the process but Cat had witnessed such circumstances before and was relieved to see her mother attempt a smile and pat the side of the bed. Jamie was sitting at the other side, his gangly frame folded into a chair, looking worried.

'I'm all right,' Jessica's voice rasped. 'Just the old trouble. I asked for a room—is that all right, darling?'

Cat nodded. Her mother's expectations hadn't diminished with their altered circumstances. Cat privately thought the company on the wards might be better than solitary splendour, but knew her mother was too old to change her ways.

'They're keeping me overnight for observation but hopefully I'll be back home tomorrow.'

'I'll stay,' Jamie volunteered with a quick flush of colour. 'You have to work, Cat.'

'There's really no need, darling,' Jessica breathed heavily, but acceded to his wishes when it was clear he had no intention of leaving. She smiled weakly in welcome when Steve Lucas popped his head round the door.

'Doctor's on his way,' he informed them. 'How are you, Jessica? Feeling any better?'

'Yes, thank you.' She beamed at him from behind the mask. 'Jamie insists on staying with me. Will you be all right on your own, Catherine? I don't like to think of you in the cottage by yourself.'

'That's easily solved. She can stay at Ranleigh, test out one of the suites.'

Jamie cast them both a knowing glance and she went red again. Cat couldn't believe her mother would put her in such an embarrassing situation. The manor house was big, but Steve Lucas's dubious protection was not something she wished to endure.

'I'd be perfectly all right at home,' she broke into what seemed like a conspiracy. Was her mother so cosily ensconced in her rosy view of life that she couldn't spot a wolf eyeing up her daughter for supper? 'But it's immaterial anyway. I can't possibly leave the hospital while you're not well.'

'Nonsense.' Her mother was unusually firm. 'You're looking tired out. . .' She ran out of words, her breathing hectic.

'I think your mother should rest, Catherine,' Steve interjected. 'I promise she'll be sensible.' He winked at Jessica Farrell who managed a weak chuckle.

The entrance of the medical team put an end to the discussion. Jamie followed them into the corridor and shifted awkwardly, sensing the tension between his sister and the older man.

'You will call if you're worried about anything, won't you?' she made him promise. He agreed, uncharacteristically giving her a hug.

Taking her elbow, Steve steered her away from the hospital room towards the exit. Catching her bleak expression, he put his arm around her shoulders in a comforting gesture.

'It's been a tough day.' His voice was warm and sympathetic. 'Do you want to go somewhere for a meal? It might help you relax.'

Cat fought the temptation to snuggle into his side. On the surface, he was being nice—considerate even. But she couldn't afford to respond; he was quite capable of ruthlessly exploiting her need for comfort. The rigid line of her shoulders rejected his touch. A tight silence developed between them, shredding Cat's nerves to breaking point.

'I don't feel hungry.' She tried to be polite. 'I'd like to go home, please.'

'Home it is.' He withdrew his arm pointedly. 'We could both use some sleep.'

'And I'm not staying at Ranleigh. Whatever my mother thinks, I'm quite capable of taking care of myself.'

'Gracious as ever,' Steve Lucas mocked her. 'I offered you the suite, not room service.'

Cat gave him a filthy look.

'You'll permit me to give you a lift back?' Steve's bland tone didn't fool her at all. He was furious.

'Have I any choice?' she muttered under her breath. His anger she was used to. She was aware of deliberately provoking him to avoid the temptation his warmth created for her.

'Well, there's a taxi rank outside. I wouldn't like to guess at the bus timetable. But if you think you're in danger of being seduced in the Range Rover, make a cabbie's day—to hell with the expense.'

'Oh, listen to Mr Outrage-and-innocence. I've never been safe with you in a confined space since the day we met,' she fired back at him. 'And you expect me to believe you have nothing on your mind but easing my mother's worries. You must think I'm a simpleton.'

Steve gave her a scathing glance. 'The fact that you don't feel safe is your own problem. I'm the one who gets slapped, bitten and scratched. All you get is cold feet and a guilty conscience.'

'I think you must be the most unpleasant man I've ever met,' she raged, her feet beating a path across the car park.

'Yeah, well, you'd take prizes for dishonesty,' he growled back, digging into his pocket and producing a key to free the lock of the Range Rover.

Cat felt ridiculous as they both swung into the Range Rover from opposite sides in almost comic unison. Neither of them was in the mood to appreciate the humour in the situation and merely shared a look of mutual irritation.

'Fasten your seatbelt,' he snapped, revving the engine with barely restrained fury before letting off the handbrake and easing out of the hospital grounds with hard-won patience.

Cat had plenty of time to reflect upon her less than generous appreciation of his help. He hadn't been obliged to find her for Jamie, he could have sent one of his minions. He had been very restrained after chasing her around the parkland of the estate and he had waited for her at the hospital, rather than leave her to find her own way home. Her hostility was a much needed defence mechanism but she was far too well brought up not to feel guilty at her lack of gratitude.

'I'm sorry.' She pushed the words past her lips when the lights of the estate came into view. 'Thank you for taking me to the hospital. . .and waiting.' She couldn't get any more fulsome than that and he merely grunted in reply.

'I hope we're not going to have another argument about where I'm going to sleep.' She brought the subject up, aggravated by his lack of response to her apology.

'No, I'm through with arguing.' His reply was cryptic but she felt relieved when they went past the manor and pulled up outside Primrose Cottage.

Getting out, she cast him a quick glance when he followed her to the door. 'I'm a bit tired for prolonged goodbyes.' She turned as the key fitted into the lock and the door swung open.

'Me too.' Steve Lucas pushed the door open, eased her inside and closed it behind them before she could draw indignant breath.

'You either get your things or I stay here with you.' He crossed his arms, surveying the condemning depths of her glare. 'And don't think I'll be insulted if when we get to Ranleigh you take your key and go straight to bed. Because, honey, I've had about as much as I can take from you today, so don't push it.'

Cat felt the slash of his gaze from her head to her toes. Her knees weakened under the blow. His eyes expressed everything there was to know about temper and she swallowed drily and turned on her heel, trying not to flee up the stairs.

Quaking inside, she hunted in her chest of drawers for nightwear and clean clothes. She was still dressed in jeans and his T-shirt, mud-splattered after her ride.

Tiredly, she pulled at her cagoul, shrugging one arm out and then the other. Catching sight of herself in the mirror, she realised that she had a smudge of mud on her face and that her hair was in tangled disarray. Dark eyes returned her inspection, tense with signals of panic in their depths.

It came as a great shock to realise that she didn't want to go to Ranleigh and go obediently to her room. What she wanted was what she feared, what she had been busily fighting against! Steve Lucas had become her source of energy; without him she was like lightning deprived of the earth. Restless fire with nothing to burn, twisting and tearing, torturing herself.

'Catherine?' Steve Lucas followed her into the room, catching sight of her reflection in the mirror. He stopped in his tracks, his jaw clenching as if he was suppressing his reaction. 'I expected to find you barricaded in.' His voice was calmer, an invitation to defuse the situation.

'I've got mud on my face.' She heard her voice, thick, almost swollen. It didn't sound like her. 'And my hair's a mess.'

Moving quietly, he turned her away from the mirror to face him. 'It doesn't matter.' His hands were warm against her upper arms, his gaze blatant with a raw sexual awareness of the signals she was giving out. 'You can have a shower at the manor house.'

'Why not here?' She couldn't tear her eyes away from his and the intensification of desire made her catch her breath.

'Because I'm here,' he growled low in his throat. 'And I'm the scheming louse that wants to take you to bed, remember.'

Reddening, she tore her gaze from his, her head bent as she whispered, 'You have some scruples, then.'

His hands tightened, squeezing the flesh on her upper arms but not hurting. 'One or two. I promised you my protection. And I think you might be in shock.'

That was true enough! She was shocked by her

reluctance to respond to his clear warning that she was
inviting trouble.

She made herself walk into the bathroom and scrub
her face with cold water. It brought her skin painfully
alive. Taking her hairbrush, she crossed the bedroom
to sit at the mirror, her senses jolting at the sight of
Steve stretched out on her bed, with his hands behind
his head.

Brushing her hair vigorously, she let her eyes wander
over his muscled frame. He had changed from the sea-
gear he had worn earlier. Denim jeans and shirt
moulded his body, a black leather jacket open, the zip
glinting in the subdued light. Powerful masculine
materials with the perfect body for their impact, sinfully adorning her white woven coverlet in a way that
should be making her spit fury.

'Do English girls' schools do a special course in
torture?' He observed her moodily from the bed.

'I don't know what you're talking about.' Her pupils
dilated at the sight of him rising up from the bed.

'Out, now!' he snapped, taking her arm and hoisting
her off the stool.

Cat was unprepared for the movement and she
unbalanced, falling against him and grabbing hold of
the lapel of his shirt. The press-studs gave and her face
skimmed the exposed breadth of his chest. Without
thinking she moved her hand down to anchor herself
and grasped the waistband of his jeans.

Steve swore under his breath, his arms closing
around her to halt her fall. There was a moment of
stunned silence when they melded together, breathing
each other's scent, Cat's face pressed into his shoulder,
her hand grazing against the zip on his jeans, his
abdomen flinching away from the intrusive thumb that
had descended beneath his waistband.

Feeling his heart triple its beat, Cat emerged from his shoulder to gaze up at him with a mouth ready to be kissed. Wrapped up in his magnetic heat, she was unable to resist the inevitable.

Steve Lucas regarded her with a grim expression. Letting her regain her balance, he stroked her hair back from her face, watching black strands imprison his flesh. Witch eyes, witch charms, such intoxicating power mixed with charismatic innocence.

'You wreck my good intentions,' he growled almost angrily. His mouth skimmed hers, making it quiver.

Cat felt his restraint like a wall between them. A fine tremor ran through him and communicated itself to her. The sheen of perspiration glistening under the shadow of stubble roughening his jaw, coupled with the wary shift of his eyes, proved him as much a victim of the moment as she was.

'I may be wrong but. . . Hell, don't do that!' he muttered as the tip of her tongue touched where his mouth had scalded in passing.

Cat's dark gaze lifted to his, soft and luminous, igniting a fierce blue flame in Steve's eyes that ate into any distant remnants of reluctance she possessed.

'Catherine?' His hands framed her face with a roughness that sketched his desperation. 'Let's be quite clear about what we're getting into here.' Steve demanded her attention, his gaze blazing with sexual intent. 'There's nothing I want more than to spread you naked across your pretty white bed. I can't take any more of you eating me up with your eyes, just to get slapped down when I take up the invitation.'

Had she really done that? Guilt momentarily clouded her expression. It was hardly surprising. He was the first man she had felt so physically drawn to but the circumstances that surrounded their tentative relationship made it well nigh impossible for the attraction to flourish. So why was she here now, being told what she was inviting and feeling the hot rush of liquid fire dissolve her bones. . .her inhibitions. . .her reason?

Unknowingly, Cat had melted against his harder frame, her thumb easing out of the constraining denim to glide under his shirt, feeling the hot damp skin flinch under her fingertips, Steve's powerful masculine lips swooping on hers, unleashing a storm of crackling electricity to sweep through her slender frame and fuse it to his.

Cat's arms wrapped around his neck, her husky murmurs of pleasure breathed out against the devilish mouth that tortured hers with a mastery of sensual expression, making her wriggle with frustration for a consummation of the need he exposed so effortlessly.

Steve licked paths of fire into her mouth, shocking her out of girlish ideas about sex and painting pictures of an erotic nature that made her blush fiercely from head to toe. The heat was unbearable and he laughed throatily as she expressed herself in a desperate whisper.

'You have to burn slowly, sweetheart; you're in too much of a hurry.'

If he had mocked her she might have reclaimed some territory, but his regard as he gathered up her hair and cooled the delicacy of her neck with a cool stream of air, seductively blown from his beautiful mouth, was miles away from mockery.

'Take my T-shirt off,' he invited smokily. 'That should cool one of us down.'

Riveted by the intensification of his gaze, washing the warm seductive charm from his features and leaving stark hunger in its wake, she fumbled for the edges of the shirt and pulled it over her head.

Steve muttered something like a prayer and pulled

her to him by the denim tabs on her jeans and undid the snap with an air of masculine purpose.

'You damn well confuse me,' he muttered, his eyes brilliant as he took in her passionate arousal, totally lacking the shamed misgivings that had marked their previous encounters. 'Why so brave now? You were nearly mute with embarrassment this morning. . .'

Cat had lost all sense of what he was saying. His thumb was brushing against her lower stomach where her jeans had parted, encouraging stings of pleasure to shiver tormentingly between her thighs. His mouth could be doing more interesting things than making meaningless noises. She wanted to unleash the hot tongues of wicked flame surging through her with brief flares of promise.

Steve tipped her chin back, knives of pleasure cutting his control to ribbons as she restlessly twisted against him as he plundered the warm silk of her throat.

'You're either a tease or the sexiest virgin in town,' he whispered into her mouth, before slipping his tongue between her neat white teeth and feeling the sweet duelling response rock him on his heels.

Lean, strong fingers ran over the lacy bra she had dried surreptitiously in the shower compartment of the *Seagull*. His breathing became laboured as his concentration was drawn from his kiss, the slow movement of his mouth lazy as he freed the front clasp of her bra and his hands cupped the firm, young curves of her breasts.

Cat's mouth flirted with his as he touched her, her lips sliding free to explore the abrasive skin of his jaw, her soft, swollen flesh enjoying the scrape of the fine bristles, her tongue tip testing and tasting, until her breathing disintegrated against his ear as his thumbs circled her nipples and the sensation made her helpless.

Suddenly, the world turned upside down! Steve picked her up and laid her down on the bed, ripping the remaining sutds on his shirt free and divesting himself of both shirt and jacket with rough haste.

Cat felt his eyes rake her body, her breasts full, the peaks spiking proudly under his searing gaze. She tensed a little as he moved closer, his arm bracing itself at the far side of her body, his big frame blotting out the light, making her feel imprisoned within the bone and muscle of his flesh. His head bent over her breasts, the light behind him flooding over his shoulders and making Cat's lashes fan down on to her cheeks as he gently nursed and nuzzled against her softness. Exquisite prickles of tension swirled around her body, taunting, teasing until she could bear it no longer. Cat had flung caution to the wind, choosing this man as her first lover, and she wanted the womanly fire inside her unleashed, to rage and be quenched in a battle as old as time. Gripping the short hair at the back of his neck, she urged him to an erotic roughness that had her squirming, moaning beneath him. His mouth ran hotly from her breastbone to her navel. Cat's stomach clenched with desire, a yelp of shock escaping from her lips, echoing around the room, making Steve bite gently, a pleased growl low in his throat as he felt her shuddering response.

'Steve,' she sobbed his name against his lips as he raised his head to soothe the sweet disarray of her senses. 'Help me, I don't know what to do. . .'

His teeth pulled at her lower lip, his tongue licking its way into her mouth. Cat clung to him as if he were a life-raft in a wide, tumultous ocean, waves breaking over her head, his lungs giving her air, only to descend again into the depths.

'Lift your hips.' He spoke huskily against her ear, his

strong hands easing the jeans down her thighs. 'Tell me what you like, angel.' His hand skimmed her stomach. 'I want you with me all the way.'

Cat hadn't a clue what she liked, except that she seemed to like everything he did to her, which seemed shockingly indiscriminate. His hand glided over her hip, dark against her thigh, making her tingle madly; some deep inner core quivered and began a throbbing demand. He pulled the thin scrap of lace guarding her loins down to join her jeans, softly stroking the inside of her thighs, feeling the muscles tremble and shiver as he moved inexorably upwards to the melting tenderness of her womanhood. Cat's body tightened into breathless expectancy, the sharp indrawn catch of her breath and soft womanly whimper accepting Steve's increasingly initimate demands upon her.

'I'm going to burn my brand so deep into your senses, you'll never want another man the way you want me.' He spoke to her almost threateningly. 'And you do want me, don't you, Catherine?' His blue eyes darkened to navy as he watched her close her eyes in an agony of need.

'Yes,' she whispered, her throat parched, arching as he aroused her body to fever pitch, his caresses intoxicating and shocking but what she wanted more than anything on earth.

The sound of the door chimes ringing crazily and followed by, 'Hello, anyone at home?' made them both freeze.

'Don't tell me that damn lock doesn't work!' Steve exclaimed with grating disbelief, his features heavy with frustration. He swore under his breath at the sound of someone moving about downstairs.

'It doesn't release the latch sometimes,' Cat admitted, her cheeks flooding with colour as she became shockingly aware of her abandoned state.

Steve's eyes raked over her body, before relinquishing her warmth, enfolding her quickly in the coverlet and going to the door.

'Cat, sweetie, are you in?' Felicity Barnhurst pushed the bedroom door open to fall back startled as Steve Lucas imposed himself in the doorway.

'Is there something I can do for you?' he asked, not in the best of tempers. Cat disappeared inside the coverlet with the feeling that she never ever want to emerge again.

'Oh, goodness, I'm terribly sorry.' Felicity sounded like a gauche schoolgirl. 'It was just Jessica. . . I wondered. . .'

'She's staying overnight in hospital. I'll give you the number of the ward so you can give them a call.' With superb mastery, he drew the woman away from the bedroom door.

Cat watched his half-naked form disappear and almost sobbed with frustration and embarrassment. Hastily pulling her clothes into place, she wondered desperately just how much Felicity had seen.

When he returned she was fully dressed, and handed him his shirt and jacket without looking at him.

'Thanks.' His voice held none of the anger she expected, merely resignation. Shrugging on his shirt, he smiled at the picture of mortification she made.

'Your reputation is in shreds,' he remarked in a deadpan tone.

'I know,' she croaked, still unable to meet his eyes. Her body was aroused and unfulfilled and she found it hard to accept that Steve Lucas wasn't exhibiting the same symptoms of frustration.

'Good thing she interrupted us really.' Steve tipped

up her chin to see the pain well into her eyes and dropped a brief soothing kiss on her mouth. 'It occurs to me that when you said you didn't know what to do, you meant it. If you haven't made love before, I think it's about time you told me.'

Twisting her head free, Cat went to pick up her overnight bag, her movements jerky and badly coordinated. 'It's hardly the sort of thing you discuss in general conversation,' she gritted, wishing they were at Ranleigh and she could close and lock her bedroom door.

'Maybe not. But if you intend to make further assaults on my jeans, I think it's something I should know.'

'Oh!' Cat's enraged growl was followed by her overnight bag aimed at his head. He ducked and she missed. Dragging every vestige of dignity she possessed, she left him to retrieve the bag and stalked out of the bedroom.

She refused to get in the Range Rover and was ignominiously shadowed by the huge machine as she forced her agitated limbs to cover the distance to the manor house. Lights went on in some of the other cottages and she felt sure that the spectacle they made would go down in Ranleigh legend. As far as her friends and acquaintances were concerned, she was Steve Lucas's lover, girlfriend—mistress! It was hard to face, but Cat was brutally honest with herself. The reason she was in a tearing fury was the fact that she wasn't, and he had welcomed the interruption! Nothing would ever make her forgive Steve Lucas for that humiliation!

CHAPTER SEVEN

CAT was up very early the next morning, a night at Ranleigh hardly conducive to sleep. Calling the hospital, she found out that her mother had had a comfortable night and was expected to return home that day.

Unable to contemplate the thought of a shared breakfast with Steve's demonic presence, she tiptoed down the wide stairs to be told by the night security man that she was not expected in the office until eleven o'clock. Her tormentor, it seemed, shared her desire to avoid an early commencement of hostilities.

She made use of the morning attending to Farrells' paperwork. Most of the horses had departed, and the empty sheds were quiet and eerie. Where once there had been bustle and activity there was now a hollow silence; even Shannon was subdued.

Going back to Primrose Cottage to shower and change, she donned a smart scarlet suit with a pretty white silk blouse. Fastening her glossy black hair back with a tortoiseshell clip, she managed to look the part of Steve Lucas's personal assistant, even if she didn't feel it.

No one knew how much it cost Cat Farrell to cross the threshold of Ranleigh that morning. Her emotions were all over the place. She felt she hated Steve Lucas but that didn't calm the deep aching demand of her body. He had succeeded in bringing the sexual tension of her ardent youth to fever pitch. Cat endured the hot racing tides of excitement as she contemplated seeing him again, only to be matched by the contrary chill of humiliation and embarrassment.

She entered his office, her legs like jelly, bracing herself for the hateful intimate knowledge she expected to see in his eyes, only to find Chas in attendance and her tormentor quite obviously preoccupied with other matters. He spared her a glance which made her blush and went on with his discussion concerning the sponsorship of the first major tournament planned for the coming year.

Frank Lucas, the president of Lucas International and Chas's grandfather, was, it seemed, expected to host the opening of Ranleigh as a golf club and leisure centre. Cat couldn't quite work out how Steve could be Chas's cousin, have the same name and not share the same grandfather, but when she was with Steve Lucas idle curiosity about his family tree was the last thing on her mind.

'Good morning, Cat.' Chas rectified the omission of greeting pointedly.

'Good morning,' she returned, casting Steve a troubled look. He had assumed his professional image, wearing a pale grey suit and light blue tie thinly striped with gold.

'Glad you could join us.' He regarded her impassively. 'How's your mother?'

She related the news gained from the hospital, finding it hard to believe this aloof stranger had reduced her to a mindless limpet the night before.

'If you need the rest of the day off, you've got it.' He picked up the phone, the leather swivel chair swinging to the side as he mentally distanced himself from them both to place his call.

'I wouldn't dream of letting you down, sir.' She

addressed his unrewarding profile and was urged to
leave the office by Chas tweaking her elbow insistently.

Chas poured her a cup of coffee and pulled his
mouth downwards expressively. 'Fallen out? It can't be
me, I haven't done anything. Not lately, anyway.'

Cat failed to reply as a leggy blonde made her way
through to Steve's office with a vague smile in their
direction.

'Michelle Williams.' Chas smiled teasingly. 'London
office. Secretary,' he added mischievously. 'Oh, Cat,'
he groaned, 'you haven't fallen for the golden boy of
Lucas-Brett. He doesn't stay around long enough to
create meaningful relationships, he's the original roll-
ing stone.'

Cat flinched from the very idea. Fallen for Steve
Lucas? Cat didn't like the idea of sexual obsession. It
sounded depraved, untouched by any ennobling
emotion. To be lost to everything but her appetite was
something she morally rejected. But what else could it
be when she was quite capable of contemplating
murder and mindless submission within the space of a
heartbeat?

'If you don't want what Steve wants, I'd give up if I
were you,' Chas prattled on, confidentially giving her
advice. 'Take it from one who knows—Steve always
gets his own way.'

Cat lifted her coffee-cup, her eyes drawn compul-
sively to the inner office. Michelle Williams was moving
around Steve, providing him with pen and a jotter as
he took down notes, receiving the faintest of winks
when she returned with a cup of coffee.

Watching, Cat found herself reluctantly absorbed. . .
and something horribly like jealousy set her teeth on
edge.

'So why did you confront him?' she pressed with

jacket to soothe her bruised skin. 'I don't want you anywhere near that horse—understand?'

Cat's lashes flickered at the sudden *frisson* of electricity coursing up her arm. His fingertip probed the sensitive veins at her wrist and she was suddenly afraid of what she was feeling, afraid of what he would see. Dark pools of emotion absorbed the man touching her, his eyes flicking briefly over the blue-black sheen of her hair and the smooth curve of her cheek. A trace of some indefinable emotion showed briefly before he drew inward again, cool mockery back in place.

Cat shivered, sensing his withdrawl and wounded by it. Her mind groped towards the essence of the problem in their relationship. While her own emotions were like a bud unfurling into full bloom, Steve was a blight, reducing the colour and perfume of such exotic maturity into a shadow of its possibilities.

'Quite right, my dear. Dangerous beast,' Colonel Cheetham confirmed, eyes twinkling at them beneath shaggy eyebrows. 'I hope we'll see you both at dinner tonight. You've received your invitation, Steven?'

'Yes, thank you. I told Penny we'd attend.' He thanked the Colonel for showing them around and steered Cat back towards the car.

'You told Penny we'd attend?' Cat queried with deceptive mildness as he joined her in the Mercedes.

'Yes.'

Cat gritted her teeth. 'Business?' she queried sweetly.

'That's right. If you don't have anything suitable to wear, buy something new and claim on expenses.'

'You're too generous.' Her voice held a husky note and his fleeting glance was ironic.

'Don't I know it! I'll take you back to the cottage.

I'll be busy for the rest of the day. I'll pick you up this evening about seven-thirty.'

'Yes, sir.' Her voice was frosted. On any other occasion, she would have indignantly accused him of trying to blur their supposed working relationship into something more personal. But her behaviour the night before gave him plenty of ammunition to shoot her down in flames if she made a protest. Besides, something had changed. She couldn't exactly say what but she was aware of new boundaries between them that hadn't existed before.

Jessica Farrell returned with Jamie that afternoon and Cat spent time making sure she was comfortable. She apologised for having to go out that night, saying that if her mother needed her she would readily make her excuses. But there was to be no reprieve there; her mother was determined to continue as normal.

Steve Lucas arrived resplendent in a dark evening suit, his jaw close-shaven, subtle aftershave giving him a familiar dynamism. He brought a large box of chocolates for her mother and courteously asked after her health, his eyes sweeping over Cat with a critical gleam.

'Are we in for a cool evening?' he enquired expressionlessly, when assisting her into the passenger seat of the Mercedes.

Cat had been on the defensive in her choice of clothes. She had chosen a flowered skirt, with a white lacy blouse and pink V-necked suede jacket. Anything that showed tantalising areas of naked skin had been hastily rejected. Soft and pink-rose romantic, she decided if he could ignore what had happened last night, so could she.

'There is a slight chill in the air,' she agreed, hating his slight smile, knowingly acknowledging the undercurrents between them.

'It's a very changeable climate. . .England's,' he offered at her swift glance sideways.

Cat wasn't in the mood to fence with him. Pointedly staring out of her side window, she endured the journey to Cheethams in virtual silence. Steve, too, seemed absorbed in his own thoughts.

Cheetham Hall was a glory to behold. It opened its doors in the summer to tourists and had beautiful gardens that were extensively used by visitors for picnic lunches. Ronald Cheetham was one of the new breed of country gentlemen who preferred prosperous elegance to genteel decay.

'I expect you're wondering why I asked you to join me at Chethams tonight?' Steve casually introduced the subject into the silence between them as the Mercedes crunched over the gravelled drive and slowed to a halt.

'It's hardly my place to question your decisions, Mr Lucas.'

He whistled softly in derision. 'Mr Lucas? Formality seems a little out of place between us, Catherine. It won't fool anybody.'

Cat remained silent. The grapevine was very effective in this little corner of Berkshire and Penelope Cheetham had ears like a bat where gossip was concerned.

There was a significant pause. Cat became suddenly conscious that his next few words were going to be of vital importance and her eyes flew to his face questioningly.

His mouth firmed with determination, his eyes direct and unwavering in intent. 'Ronald Cheetham wants a deal with Ranleigh over providing rides for guests. He also thinks it would add prestige to his school for young hopefuls if you managed the riding school.'

Cat was absolutely astonished. 'But——'

'I haven't finished,' he cut her protest dead, his voice firm and authoritative. 'Together with that we're prepared jointly to sponsor your show-jumping career, which your reputation suggests will enhance the school's name and put Cheethams firmly on the map.' Opening the car door, he came around to let her out, noting the fulminating anger in her dark gaze. 'It also means you can shed the role as my assistant far more quickly than you could if you were waiting for the go-ahead for stables at Ranleigh. Think about it,' he advised. 'If you stay with me, two weeks from now we'll be in New York, a month later mainland Europe.'

Stunned speechless, Cat was unable to vent her feelings about this sudden change in her fortunes. She was bewildered at the speed of events. Steve Lucas wasn't a man to waste time! It hadn't occurred to her that the Cheethams' tour would lead to anything like this! The sponsorship of her show-jumping career was a dream come true but it was being used to squash any objections she might make to the permanent demise of Farrells.

Angrily, she wondered what her escort would do if she threw the cat among the pigeons and decided to go to New York with him. Probably use Primrose Cottage as his wild card. He knew all her vulnerabilities. Cheetham's was the only deal she was going to get! He had told her on the eve of the formal dinner invitation so that she had no time to rant and rave.

Penelope Cheetham stood in the reception area with her silver-haired father, her gaze taking in every detail of Cat's appearance.

'Goodness, darling, what a pretty outfit. You look about fifteen.' Claws out, she was looking for blood.

Dressed in a black, slinky, off-the-shoulder dress,

Penelope looked sophisticated and very much a woman. 'Steve must feel like a positive cradle-snatcher.'

Reeling from Steve's announcement, Cat felt as if she had been clipped on the jaw. She couldn't believe Penelope had actually said that, linked them so openly as a couple.

'I find a mixture of purity and passion intoxicating,' Steve returned, not the least put out. 'You look exquisite, Penny. I hope you've recovered from your fall yesterday.'

'Oh, that.' She was off-hand. 'I should have taken Daddy's advice.' She hugged her father's arm and he regarded her indulgently. 'Blood Star is a brute. Fortunately, the bruising isn't where anyone can see.'

Steve smiled and drew Cat away as other guests arrived. She saw with a sinking heart that Felicity Barnhurst was regarding them with round eyes and wished she could sink into the floor.

'Purity and passion,' Cat muttered with loathing, finding her voice.

'If you're going to dress like a Sunday School teacher, someone has to defend you. Being found on your bed with a half-naked man isn't going to go away just because you dress as if you've never heard the word "sex".'

Crumpling inwardly with mortification, two red spots of colour in her cheeks, she allowed him to provide her with sherry.

'And just how long have you been negotiating with Colonel Cheetham?' she demanded in a furious undertone, determined not to let him distract her from the real issue.

'Later, sweetheart. We don't want to argue in public now, do we?'

Cat suddenly became aware of the interest they were creating and contained herself with difficulty. She was glad when Henry Winterton came over to greet her and Steve drifted from her side to greet a business acquaintance.

'How's Oxford?' she queried without any real interest, knowing that he could talk for hours with only the necessity of mere nods and the occasional word from her.

'How's life at Ranleigh? It sounds much more interesting.' His gaze glittered over her assessingly and Cat realised with a sinking heart that the estate had become something of a talking point, not the least of its notoriety surrounding herself and her cheat of an employer.

'I must say, Cat, I never thought you'd get banned from my mother's tea-table. Flick and Penny are serving a life sentence. I'm running out of young gels to take home.'

Cat failed to see the humour of the situation. Her friends were hideously insensitive to her feelings, because for them life and love were a game. Penelope Cheetham had her eye on Steve Lucas and the fact that he'd been supposedly snatched from under her nose by 'nice' Cat Farrell was seen as a gem worthy of recounting throughout the county.

Steve courteously seated her at the dinner-table and she froze as he drew her dark curtain of hair back over her shoulders, while responding to a remark from Ronald Cheetham. It was a gesture of understated possession that provided fuel for a battery of meaningful glances around the table.

'I hate you,' she muttered under her breath, as he leaned close to catch her words.

'Don't be cruel, darling. If I ignored you, it would

look as if I ditched you after a one-night stand. I don't want people to think I'm heartless.'

Fiddling with her knife, Cat counted to ten. 'You've successfully ignored me all day. I'm surprised you feel the need to maintain appearances.' She regretted the whispered reproach as soon as it was spoken but Steve chose not to hear her.

If he was pressurising her into accepting the Cheetham deal, he couldn't employ more effective tactics. She had to get away from him. Even now, when she was smarting from his cool amusement, she was terribly aware of every move he made.

Places were set for twelve. The dining-room was ornate, the table Victorian, polished to gleam, the chandelier above casting shards of light on to the glitter of glass and silver below.

Ronald Cheetham and his daughter took up their positions as host and hostess. The Colonel was a widower of some ten years and the absence of a mother's influence and consequently a father's over-indulgence had a decided effect on Penelope's character. She was positively dripping venom and Cat tensed as if awaiting a blow. She didn't have long to wait.

'What do you think about Daddy's idea for the riding school, Cat?' Penny stopped the conversation around them, her tone suggesting there was more to it than idle enquiry.

'Penelope,' her father began crustily, 'don't be so impetuous, the idea's still in its early stages.'

'I think it's a wonderful idea. Cat needs sponsorship and if Steve is willing to buy her a first-class horse, she should be winning everything in sight in a year.'

Steve Lucas didn't turn a hair, his hand coming to rest over Cat's in silent restraint. 'I'm afraid I wouldn't know a good horse from a donkey. Your father's agreed to consult with Catherine about any new purchase, which will come out of the money designed to boost the riding school's profile. You mustn't confuse generosity with business, sweetheart—the two don't mix.'

A titter of laughter went around the dinner-table, Penelope Cheetham's insinuation that Steve Lucas was acting as Cat's sugar-daddy dealt with neatly and rebounding on its perpetrator in a way that subdued further mud-slinging.

'Yes. . . Er—Steven and I are looking to add Catherine's talent to Cheetham's riding school but it's up to the young lady. I'm sure Catherine wants time to think the idea over.'

Cat smiled vaguely at the expectant looks she received, but inside her blood was boiling. 'It's an attractive offer,' was her only comment. Fortunately the conversation picked up again and she was off the hook.

Cat drew on unknown sources of endurance to get through the evening. Felicity Barnhurst had been cornered in the powder-room and stammered a quick apology, seeing the murderous light in her friend's eyes.

'I'm sorry, Cat. I wouldn't have said anything, only Penny was being so bitchy about you, I. . .' She giggled nervously. 'It really took the wind out of her sails, I can tell you.'

Cat failed to feel gratified. Telling Felicity exactly what she thought of her didn't help either. She stayed behind when Felicity made her escape, sitting on one of the padded stools in front of a vanity mirror. The face that looked back at her was eloquent with feeling. Could you love, hate and desperately want someone all at the same time? She had no one to ask. She was so used to protecting her mother that she couldn't imagine asking her for advice on so sensitive an issue.

Steve reclaimed her as the party broke up, coming up behind her and taking her arm. 'It's time we were going, darling. Are you ready?'

If he called her 'darling' one more time, she thought she'd explode. She didn't resist the gentle pressure against her elbow urging her forward, as she had no desire to stay any longer at Cheethams.

Once inside the Mercedes, Cat sat in frigid silence. The whole evening had been a nightmare. She had known most of the people there all her life, yet tonight she had felt transformed before their very eyes.

'Penelope Cheetham is a nasty piece of work,' Steve commented eventually with a glance sideways. 'Did she upset you?'

Cat twisted around in her seat to view him with disbelief. 'Penny's an amateur compared to you! Tell me, was I the last to know about your plans for Cheetham's? You really are a devious, unprincipled swine. And to think, most of the people there tonight believe we're lovers! You've even managed to get me banned from the vicarage!' She almost choked with outrage.

Steve Lucas's mouth curled into a smile. 'Poor Henry. He'll have to find someone else to parade before his strait-laced parents.'

'I'm glad you're amused.' Cat felt her brittle control was close to snapping. 'I value my reputation. Old-fashioned, I suppose, but the idea that I'm your mistress, being given presents, I find humiliating.'

Steve flicked on the wipers as a spatter of raindrops obscured the windscreen.

'I doubt people who know you would think that,' he returned evenly.

'You did,' she pointed out. 'What was it you accused me of being—an amateur gold-digger?' In fact, you considered Chas an idiot if he didn't demand my body in exchange for a favourable contract.'

He winced. 'OK. But the circumstances were different. I fully accept you're a decent, hard-working, conscientious young woman who deserves the chance I'm giving you to make my investment good. Pure business, nothing personal. You make a lousy personal assistant, by the way—I can only justify keeping you on in that capacity as stress relief—an executive toy.'

Stress relief! An executive toy! Light entertainment while he was in the UK. It became crystal-clear why he had been so distant that day. Finding out she was a virgin had made him reassess the situation. He was moving out fast. She was now 'decent', 'hard-working' and 'conscientious'. A far cry from the gold-digger and tease he had accused her of being in the past.

'I seem to have gone up in your estimation. I wonder why.'

'You know why,' Steve Lucas grated, sounding as if he was tightly controlling his responses. 'My conscience. . .' He cast her a glance at her audible sneer. 'I do have one, Catherine, whatever you may think. It tells me you're not ready for the kind of relationship I want.'

'And what exactly do you want?' she challenged him, temper numbing her usual sense of caution.

Steve brought the Mercedes to a smooth halt outside Primrose Cottage. Releasing his seatbelt, he turned, leaning his arm against the back of his seat regarding her with assessing masculine interest.

'I want an affair.' It was hardly news but the baldness of the statement was faintly shocking. 'I spent all night thinking about it. . .' He smiled but his eyes were seductive as they monitored the emotions flitting over her expressive features. 'Not sex,' he moderated, 'you. I realise, with your lack of experience, you might want more out of a relationship than it's possible for me to give.'

Cat agreed but found his businesslike approach to negotiations a little hard to swallow. With her newly fledged emotions barely acknowledged, to have Steve practically outline the rules of play was something that hurt unbearably.

'Is this little talk supposed to ease your conscience?' she enquired huskily. 'It sounds as though you want to take me to bed and say "I told you so" if I'm naïve enough to develop any emotional commitment to you.'

He had the grace to look uncomfortable with that. 'It's the way I live. I'm going to be in the UK for two months out of the next six. After that, it depends on the board's policy decisions. I can't promise forever, Catherine. I've been on my own for too long to take on board passengers. I'm not going to lie to you, I want you to know how it is.'

Cat viewed him with disbelief. 'I think I would have preferred it if you had lied. You're offering me the chance to make a fool of myself and know it! How callous can you get?'

Shrugging, he hunched into the driver's seat, looking out into the darkness. 'Love is a very fleeting thing. I think that's the one thing I don't want to teach you. If I'm wrong and you could handle that kind of relationship, tell me. If not, quit while you're ahead.'

'You're very bitter, Steve.' She almost pitied him. Almost but not quite. He was destroying her with every word.

He turned to look at her, his dark lashes fringing his eyes, the pain in their depths living on the air between them. 'There's no kind of love you can ever guarantee, Catherine.' A wry smile alleviated his expression. 'You almost make me believe in Santa Claus and the tooth fairy. . . You still have dreams, and I want you to keep them—but I want you more.' His voice became hard and driven and Cat felt her blood heat in response.

'Use and be used?' She summed up his terms. 'No illusions on either side.'

'Put starkly. . .yes.' Steve's finger traced the under-curve of her mouth, his blue eyes heavy-lidded and intent. Caught in the web of his desire, Cat felt herself relax, her lips parting as his wayward finger softly and coaxingly explored the velvety texture. He would be a wonderful lover, her thoughts besieged her. Meeting his gaze, the sensual satisfaction she saw there snapped her back into cold reality. He had made her body his ally and he knew it! His get-out clause wasn't honesty, it merely justified the poverty of his emotions.

'That sounds just your sort of relationship.' She jerked her face away to avoid his disturbing touch. His terms were preposterous and yet the temptation to throw caution to the wind was almost overwhelming. She summoned up the strength to deny him.

'You're right.' She freed the door at her side of the car. 'I'm not ready for that!' Her contempt was blistering.

'We'll meet at breakfast.' Steve's bones set in a hard mask. Self-denial wasn't something he practised often or liked the taste of.

'I'll give you the file on Cheetham's, see what you think of the proposals. You can negotiate any amend-ments while I'm away. When you've cooled down you might find the deal quite advantageous.'

'Don't count on it,' she muttered, biting back the question that leapt to her lips. Despite her anger, the thought of him leaving made her heart plummet. She was incapable of responding to his casual 'gooodnight'.

Slotting her key into the door of the cottage, she only looked back when she heard the Mercedes move off towards Ranleigh. Cat felt fatally wounded. She had fallen in love with a sexual opportunist, who primed his victim and then laid down rules to avoid any messy emotional entanglement. She had been warned! She would be a fool to get any further involved with such a cynical man.

The mellow, tranquil atmosphere of Primrose Cottage did nothing to soothe her riotous senses. She felt like a stranger in her own home. The whole evening had been like that. Among the county set, Cat Farrell was no longer a young girl, shouldering her family's responsibilities. She had been reintroduced as Steve Lucas's mistress. She had become a stranger to her friends and, worst of all, with the host of conflicting emotions inside her, she had become a stranger to herself!

CHAPTER EIGHT

BREAKFAST was served in Steve's own suite of rooms. Cat was shown the way by a well groomed receptionist she recognised as an inhabitant of Baron's Green. Her cheeks tinged with colour as Steve came to the door in the process of fastening his shirt. She deliberately avoided the expanse of hair-roughened chest to be taunted by the intimate gleam in his eyes singling her out as an object of desire. He had given her his terms and was back on the prowl!

'Thank you, Sheila.' He dismissed the receptionist and opened the door wider. 'Coming in?'

'Wouldn't you prefer me to wait until you've finished dressing?' Cat wished she could achieve cold sarcasm but her voice broke revealingly.

Steve's quick intelligence picked up on her discomfort. 'Why so shy? The other night we were both——'

Her eyes skidded away from his. 'You wanted to discuss Cheetham's,' she cut in desperately. 'I could read through the file while you——'

'Make myself decent.' A roguish smile took in the flush on her cheeks and the delicate quiver of her mouth. 'Good idea.'

He gestured at a desk placed near the window, the door open nearby revealing a tumbled bed. Cat felt her eyes straying from one danger zone to another. He seemed to have had a restless night. She knew how that felt: she had been tortured by a terrible craving through the wolf hours and beyond. Her eyes itched with tiredness.

She tried to concentrate on the neatly typed pages in front of her. The case was put, very succinctly, that the sort of clientèle Ranleigh would appeal to would prefer the Cheetham set-up to a more modest venture should they wish to indulge in equine pursuits. Costings for a new stable at Ranleigh were expensive and not recommended.

'It's all sewn up, isn't it?' she demanded bleakly, looking up to see him fastening his tie with absent attention. He was watching her. To be precise, his gaze had been occupied with the slim lines of her calf and the delicate hollows of her ankle revealed by her light sandal.

'I'm willing to listen to any reasonable objections.' The heavy undertow of sexual appreciation remained stamped on his features. 'The Colonel doesn't want a new competing business to grow up on his doorstep. He knows you're the only valuable assett Farrells had. Merging talents and resources makes sense.' He moved closer, standing over her as she tried to escape him by pretending to be engrossed in the document. 'This is your future. I want you to iron out any problems and have it ready to discuss with me next Saturday.'

'It won't be the same. . .' She tried to get in touch with her old fervency about the stables but it wasn't the rebirth of Farrells that was firing her. 'You just want to destroy it all, don't you? For some reason you want to detach Ranleigh from its past. . . I'm surprised you haven't flattened the manor house. You probably would if Frank Lucas would let you!'

He leaned down to place his hands on the arms of the chair, his face alight with sensual challenge. The hard bones were locked in a mask of desire that she easily recognised.

'I don't have to ask anyone for permission,

Catherine. And this has nothing to do with Ranleigh. I'll be leaving in an hour. When I'm gone, maybe you'll be able to think straight and realise when you're on to a good thing.'

'Will I?' Everything womanly in her wanted to challenge his masculine arrogance. Rising, she made him move back but not much. He was standing close enough to kiss and was doing it on purpose.

'What's the matter, Steve?' she taunted. 'Do you want someone to kiss you goodbye?'

'Another word and I'll take you in there.' His head flicked towards the bed. 'And we both know you won't fight.'

'Do we?' Hearing a rustle outside the door, she was confident enough of rescue to fight back. She straightened his tie, her eyes flicking provocatively up to his, her fingertips tingling from his warmth as they brushed his chest. 'I'd want more than an hour, Steve.' She kissed the base of his chin and looked to the door with satisfaction when Michelle Williams poked her head around after a brief knock.

'The car will be ready. . . Oh, sorry.' The blonde grinned. 'Excuse me.'

'You're excused.' Steve barely waited for her to leave before he bent his head, neatly subduing Cat's attempt to follow the other woman from the room by pulling her into his body and taking her mouth with devastating purpose.

The kiss wrenched away any pretence Cat had of being in control of the situation. The tender curves of her mouth were devoured with a hunger that made her mind spin away into a vortex of unquenched fire. Her legs weakened, the soft curves of her buttocks coming into contact with the hard edge of the desk, Steve's thigh forcing its way in between her knees, tormenting the aching need in her loins with the aroused thrust of his.

As he tore his mouth from hers, Steve's hands very deliberately plucked the buttons of her blouse free. Heat scalded his cheekbones, his eyes brilliant with blue fire.

'You're on borrowed time, do you know that?' His hand surged over her breast, his head dipping to bite at the creamy exposed curve making her head fall back, his arm behind her back her only support. Cat heard her protests turn to whimpers of pleasure. He was so much stronger than she was and she didn't really want to fight.

'Steve. . .' she sobbed his name, burying her face in his shirt when he pulled her back into his arms and held her with obvious restraint, his body shuddering with the shock of flashfire emotion.

'One thing you don't do,' he groaned into her silky black hair, 'is tease a man who wants you as badly as I do. Not if you want to keep your virginity for some knight in shining armour.'

'I suppose you. . .you didn't plan this cosy break-fast.' She tried to recover, her dark eyes showing all the signs of aftershock that were mirrored in his.

'You were right. My good intentions disappeared in the night. I wanted kissing goodbye.' He smiled with real charm, making an attempt to refasten her buttons before she eased away from him, turning away to complete the task, her cheeks flooding with hot colour.

'I'd. . .I'd better go.' Her eyes skittered to his and then to the phone as it began to ring.

'Catherine, I've been thinking——'

'I'll see you next week.' With a bright stabbing glance she took in his handsome features, which showed a sensuality that made her bones melt, and literally ran from the room.

'He's free, then, is he?' Michelle Williams passed her in the corridor, showing no signs of surprise at Cat's inarticulate murmur as she fled down the stairs or her boss's frustrated roar of the girl's name as he inserted himself in the doorway to see his prey fleeing as if her life depended on it.

Cat watched the bulldozers flatten the tack-room with an intense pang of regret and nostalgia for what had been. Chas approached with a bottle of champagne and two glasses.

'To the future,' he suggested, putting a friendly arm around her shoulders.

The future was a dark tunnel of uncertainty for Cat. Two days had passed, during which she must have thought of Steve Lucas a million times.

'I suppose the occasion should be marked.' She allowed him to pour champagne into her glass, sadly viewing the huge cleats of mud dug up by the bulldozers' tracks. It was hard to believe that in a few months' time the grass would be as smooth as a billiard table and nothing would hint that Farrells had even existed.

'Congratulations, Steve,' she toasted to the west. If anyone had told her a month ago that she would stand and watch Farrells be demolished without lifting a finger, she would have scoffed in disbelief.

'Now you know what it's like to have Steve re-route your life, you might have some sympathy for me.' Chas clinked his glass against hers.

Cat rescued the iron engraved name plate belonging to the stables and walked with Chas back towards Ranleigh and its perimeter fringe of cottages. They both stood back from the road when a red Ferrari cruised up alongside them. The stylish vehicle slowed down significantly and Chas went white and then bright red as the car accelerated into the courtyard.

'Good God, it's Serena!' he exclaimed, thunderstruck.

'Serena Hamilton?' Cat frowned. 'Well, isn't that good?'

'Good?' Chas repeated as if he didn't understand the word. 'Last time I saw her, she threw my ring back at me.' Quickening his pace, he gave Cat an apologetic smile. 'I think Pop Hamilton prefers the idea of Steve as a son-in-law to me. If Serena's slipped her minders, all hell will break loose in the next twenty-four hours, and guess who'll get the blame?'

Cat felt her whole body go cold. What had Steve Lucas got to do with Serena? He had talked about her in a way that clearly indicated he thought she was too good for Chas. But he had never so much as hinted that he was interested in the girl himself. Why would he? She scorned her blinkered vision. He had been too busy trying to get the better of her to sour his efforts by mentioning other commitments.

'Is that why you pretended we were romantically attached?' Cat asked with sudden enlightenment. 'To pretend you didn't care about Steve and Serena?'

Chas looked guilty, darting her an apologetic look. 'Not exactly. I wanted him to know how it felt to. . . er—want a woman out of his reach. He doesn't love Serena. He just wants Hamilton money.'

Deciding treachery ran in the family, Cat gave him a speaking look and left him to face the onslaught of the Lucas clan. As Chas predicted, limousines pulled up at regular intervals decanting various members of his family. Serena, it turned out, had been visiting London

to shop at Harrods with her godmother, Sylvia Lucas.
Sylvia Lucas was Steve's mother!

Cat had become briefly acquainted with the older
woman when she had visited Ranleigh to ask Michelle
Williams to type up some notes for her.

'So you're Jessica's daughter,' had been her brief
comment after a vinegary inspection. 'Beautiful too.'
It had sounded like condemnation.

To add to the circus, Lee Hamilton arrived by
helicopter and the president of Lucas-Brett, Frank
Lucas, was expected on the morrow.

'Pretty heavy stuff,' Chas informed her. 'Serena says
she's here to see Steve. No one but me believes her.'
He was glum. 'Pop Hamilton thinks I'm a worthless
playboy.'

Cat kept tactfully silent.

'You try growing up under the shadow of Steve "Mr
Perfect" Lucas,' he blurted out resentfully. 'Or should
I say Brett? He took up every chance my grandfather
gave him and came out with honours. I just don't have
the same hunger for success. I didn't inherit his
demons.'

Cat was confused. 'Brett,' she repeated, frowning.
She had always assumed the Brett part of Lucas-Brett
had been bought out by the Lucases.

'Yes, that's his mother's name. She married my uncle
when Steve was ten. He adopted Steve and changed
his name. When he died my grandfather saw Steve's
potential and became his mentor. Steve went on his
own for a while, started Brett Enterprises. Lucas-Brett
was the result of a very successful merger. Steve and
Frank are as thick as thieves.'

That explained why Steve Lucas always called Frank
Lucas Chas's grandfather, but it left a lot unsaid. She
remembered his hints at a less than secure childhood

and wondered if that was why he found the timeless complacency of Ranleigh's inhabitants so irksome.

Cat managed to put the dramas of Ranleigh behind her during the next week. She studied Colonel Cheetham's proposal, noting with surprise that the investment to be put into the stables was considerable. She made a detailed analysis of what was on offer, suggesting adjustments to be made, and began a tentative relationship with Blood Star.

The magnificent black thoroughbred had a beautiful clean pair of heels. He needed a rider with the right sense of timing and he would be a master of the show-jumping arena.

At the back of her mind, it niggled away that there was more to her sudden desire to succeed with Blood Star than just mastering an excellent competition horse. For one thing, Steve Lucas had forbidden her to ride him, and even more deplorable was the slight suspicion that she would enjoy Penelope Cheetham's green face as Cat tamed a horse that had thrown her and bruised more than her pride.

After a week of making the stallion's acquaintance, she began riding the horse over the surrounding countryside, attending to the grooming afterwards herself. He was spirited but manageable, and four days later she felt the time had come to try Blood Star over the jumps.

Several of the stable lads came to watch her put the ebony thoroughbred through its paces. She didn't see the silver Mercedes cruise into the stableyard; she was concentrating on getting Blood Star to complete the circuit in the paddock.

Steve Lucas ducked out of the sleek vehicle as she straightened up the stallion to approach the last fence.

A sound like a gunshot rent the air and Blood Star went straight through the mock construction and wheeled sharply at the paddock fence, snorting and rearing up, with Cat holding on for dear life. The horse came back down on to four legs, charged the gate and cleared it, rearing up in the courtyard, trying to dislodge the woman fighting for control.

Steve Lucas swore under his breath. 'What the hell is she doing on that horse?' he bit out tensely at Ronald Cheetham.

'It was the sound of the starting pistol. Cat had Blood Star eating out of her hand. She has the measure of that horse. I can't argue with her professional judgement.'

'Well, I sure as hell can. If there's anything left of her to argue with,' Steve hissed furiously.

'She's gentling him. Don't go near!' He caught the younger man's sleeve as he would have gone forward, and Steve forced himself to watch, knowing he could make matters worse if he spooked the horse, barely pacified by the fact that Cat was slowly bringing the beast under her control.

'I hope she's got some stamina because she'll have me to gentle afterwards,' he muttered under his breath, his eyes riveted on the meld of woman and horse. 'And it'll take more than a few soft words.'

Cheetham actually smiled, receiving a glare for his trouble, and nodded at one of the stable lads, who approached carefully and caught the bridle.

Cat blew a stream of air up into her fringe. 'Phew, what a temper!' She patted the horse's lathered neck, for the first time becoming aware of Steve's presence. So he was back! She frowned at the glitter of fury in his eyes. He didn't look any more appealing than the demonic Blood Star.

'Get off that horse, now!' The low pitch of his voice carried with surprising force and Cat swallowed drily, responding inwardly to the threat he posed.

'He'll think he's won if I——'

'Get off or I'll drag you off!'

She didn't doubt that he meant it. Neither did any of the spectators. You could hear a pin drop.

Flushing with anger, she dismounted stiffly, black eyes eloquent with humiliated anger. Undoing her chin-strap, she gave the stable lad instructions, shaking her hair free in a casual gesture, trying to pretend she was unmoved by his fury.

'I'll speak to you later, Colonel. Catherine, I'm taking you back to Ranleigh. Get in the car.'

Another order! She viewed him with a militant glare. He would regret playing the heavy-handed lover quite so publicly when he learnt that Miss Moneybags was staying at the manor.

Deciding to avoid a public fight, she stalked proudly to the silver Mercedes, her skin drawn tight over her finely boned features. Steve followed her, barely restrained energy sizzling like a force-field around him.

'Whatever's the matter?' She pretended an innocence she didn't feel. Steve Lucas did not like being thwarted and she had become a persistent thorn in his flesh.

'I'll tell you what's the matter, at length, when we get home.' He spoke through his teeth. 'You're on very thin ice, lady, so I suggest you keep that provocative little mouth of yours shut.'

Cat was impressed despite herself. There was a savagery about his anger that an expensive grey business suit and crisp white linen shirt did little to civilise.

'It was nothing I couldn't handle,' she offered in a subdued voice, quelled from further speech by the

black-tempered invective that was as insulting as it was
heavy with feeling.

When they reached Ranleigh, Cat tried to walk
away, having had quite enough of his foul mood. Steve
caught up with her and unceremoniously propelled her
into the front porch of Ranleigh Manor. She was
directed up the oak staircase, a handful of her jacket
in Steve Lucas's fist.

'I don't know what you think you're doing!' she fired
up, trying to stop him locking the door, noting with
panic that she was in his suite of rooms for the second
time.

'I thought I told you not to go near that horse!' He
brushed her hands away, pocketing the key. 'You could
have been killed, you little fool. What the hell are you
trying to prove?'

'Why do I have to be proving anything?' she yelled
back at him. 'Blood Star belongs to Colonel Cheetham.
If he gives me permission to ride him, what has it got
to do with you?'

Steve's blue eyes flayed her. 'It's got everything to
do with me. If I'm going to invest in your future, I'll
make damn sure it's going to be long and prosperous,
not thrown away so you can show you're a hot-shot in
the saddle.'

Trembling with rage, Cat felt her battened-down
emotions rise in a sudden wave of feeling. It almost felt
good to yell and rage: it released some of the pain of
the days she had spent without sight of him.

'If I break my neck you won't have to worry about
investing. I'm not going to win anything on a damn
rocking-horse, so if you're serious about sponsoring me
you'll just have to butt out.' She deliberately used
American slang to make her point succinctly.

'You won't get a cent out of me to ride that stallion.

Maybe mated with a docile mare it might produce a foal with the skill and right temperament, but that's all it's good for. In the arena, a flashlight or a kid crumpling a candy paper would send you crashing through every obstacle in sight.'

'Nonsense.' She pushed a distraught hand through her hair, lifting the heavy weight from her heated neck. 'A gunshot is hardly usual——'

'It's not a risk I'm prepared to take.' His eyes skimmed the pale curve of her exposed neck. 'Let's stick to business. You need my money, you ride what I tell you to ride.'

'Your money?' She snapped to attention, her dark eyes widening with dawning realisation. 'I thought it belonged to the company.'

'I do make personal investments. Cheetham's isn't a big enough concern to interest Lucas-Brett.'

'I don't want your money! You're not going to mould my life in that way, Steve. God.' She laughed bitterly. 'That says it all about you, doesn't it? You can pay out the dollars but, when it comes to your emotions, you're bankrupt.'

His gaze was as brilliant and hard as a diamond. 'If I was trying to buy you, Catherine, I wouldn't have refused what was so blatantly on offer before I left.'

'Wouldn't you?' She threw caution to the winds. 'But then that clever brain would have worked out that taking the local virgin wouldn't have raised your credit with Lee Hamilton. You could hardly criticise Chas for his behaviour, when yours was equally reproachable.'

His nostrils flared, and his jaw clenched angrily. 'What the hell has Hamilton got to do with anything?'

'Why don't you ask him? He and the rest of your family are here, led by his daughter Serena who appears to be looking for you.'

'Serena's here?'

'Yes.' Her lip wobbled despite her resolve that it shouldn't. Steve looked poleaxed. 'I believe you're ahead in the stakes for society wedding of the year. I suppose not being a *bona fide* Lucas means you have to marry well. So, now you've got other fish to fry, maybe I could go home. This particular soap opera leaves me cold.'

Dark lashes hooded his expression. 'Serena's a pretty girl,' he considered, his words slicing into her like a knife. 'Sweet, warm temperament, heiress to a fortune. Doesn't have a shrewish bone in her body or a tendency to make me part with large amounts of money for the pleasure of being tortured by unsatisfied lust.'

'Why, you——!'

Catching her hand, he dragged her to him, one arm fastening like a steel band around her waist, the other imprisoning her fingers in the crushing strength of his.

'You were saying.' His breath crashed against her cheek, his heartbeat pounding against her breast. 'Or were you just hoping if you threw enough stones I'd retaliate the way you want me to?'

'I don't know what you——' Her mouth was crushed under his without tenderness or mercy. Masculine lips roughly persuaded Catherine to allow him entry to the moist sensuality within. She tried to resist, straining against him, but he held her so tightly, the dark storm of his kisses upsetting her breathing and making her fight for air to break the seal of his mouth against hers. When she succeeded, his teeth nipped her earlobe, his tongue slipping into the shell, making her shiver with reaction.

Reclaiming her mouth, he let go of her fingers, his hand sliding over the front of her suede waistcoat, releasing the buttons from their eyelets. Cupping her breast through her brightly printed blouse, he caressed her with increasing urgency, muttering frustratedly against her lips.

'If you think I'm going to let you break your bones on that hell-born horse, you're crazy.' An ungentle bite at her lower lip made her squirm against him. Steve winced as she clutched a handful of his hair. Her teeth were ready to bite back and for a moment there was a space between them that bristled with animosity.

Cat's pulses hammered, his anger dangerous and darkly exciting. Their breath mingled, her face pale, neck aching as she tried to maintain some distance and evade that devilish mouth.

'Is this your idea of keeping me safe?' she scorned him, shaken by her depth of response and desperate to camouflage it.

'Why not?' He viewed her heaving breasts, felt the taut plane of her stomach and the cushioned flesh of her thighs straining against him with mounting excitement. 'Wanting me is making you reckless. I couldn't live with myself if you got hurt for the want of a simple solution.'

'No!' Cat shuddered as his arms tightened, her curves moulding to his as she was lashed against his body.

'No?' His hungry lips plundered her throat, finding all the sensitive spots, pressing against the urgent pulse shielded by silken skin. 'Tell me again, Catherine. Tell me how much you hate this.'

She didn't hate it at all! Steve moved against her, demanding the ease of her flesh, the message simple, sensual and seducing.

His gaze stripped her of pretence. The rumpled state of her clothes matching the rumpled state of her emotions. His hands framed her face, drinking in the swollen passion of her lips and the glazed heat of her eyes. Hair as black as night tumbled around his hands, curling inside her collar in dramatic contrast to the paleness of her skin.

Cat's fingers crept up to cover his, but his mouth seduced her senses into doing nothing more than admire their lean strength. The raw silk of his tongue was doing indecent things in her mouth and she ached for the fulfilment she had denied herself, her body alive with half formed wants and desires. She spasmed with desire when Steve bit into the join of her neck, her legs nearly giving way.

'This has been the longest week of my life,' he growled into her mouth. 'I thought that crazy horse was going to kill you.'

His words were another blow to Cat's threadbare resistance. Steve sounded shaken. It felt as if he cared. Her love flowered like a seed in the desert.

Lifting her up, he took her through into the bedroom, following her down on to the bed, wrenching his tie free and undoing his shirt. Unbidden, Cat took advantage of the newly exposed territory. Pushing the shirt off his shoulders, she kissed the salty exposed breadth of his chest, helpless to resist as his brown fingers slid the buttons of her blouse free.

For a moment, embarrassment flooded back. Stirring, she felt the swift return of his gaze to her face. Steve was a stranger. No longer angry, his eyes burnt with a fever, his face intent, all expression consumed by the primitive force driving him on. Reaching out to her, he pulled her to him, ridding her of her blouse, kissing her as he unhooked her bra, letting her bury her face into his neck as he threw aside the lacy garment and cupped her aching breasts in his hands.

'I need you.' The harshly spoken words startled her. Steve pushed her back on to the bed, suddenly lacking the smooth assurance of control. Cat's fingers tightened apprehensively on his shoulders as he bent over her, capturing one dusky nipple between his lips, hearing her guttural moan as he mouthed and nipped at her fiercely, rousing her body to match the urgency of his.

The sound of a car outside and the bright chatter of voices reminded her of Serena's presence in the house.

'Stop it,' she panted. 'Steve, I can't. . .' Her eyes fluttered closed as he traced the creamy curve of her stomach. Moving restlessly, she let him loosen her jodhpurs, shaking as his fingers lightly eased a path between her trembling thighs.

'I'm not going to hurt you.' His voice was roughened by his response to touching her, acknowledging the tension in her body.

'You will,' she sobbed, knowing it wasn't physical pain that menaced her—that would be almost welcome. She yearned endlessly for his love.

The dark storm of his anger had faded away, his mouth coaxing, words whispered to heat her blood, his tongue making lightning forays into her mouth before tasting the damp perspiration trickling down her throat. His hands skimmed her body, creating silken pathways of pleasure, his touch delicate and sure, drawing Catherine into a golden web of desire that tangled endlessly around her.

Eyes black behind a veil of lashes, Cat felt the hot brush of his lips travel over her skin, felt the flame of his tongue dip into her navel and the burning ache of her loins throb an urgent message throughout her slim, restless body.

Shockwaves crashed over her. Steve's bronzed shoulders gleamed and rippled, his forearms roughened with hair, abrasive against her skin as he wrapped himself around her lower limbs, the scorch of his mouth

inside her hipbone making her body clench with an
agony of arousal.

Just as Cat felt her control disintegrating into mindless delight, Steve rose above her, his mouth tender
against hers. Her fingers slid over his muscled biceps to
his shoulders as his heat enveloped her.

'You like flirting with danger, don't you, Catherine?'
Steve's whispered growl was barely audible as her soft
lips cushioned the sound.

'Yes. . .' Her thoughts escaped her. If danger was
this man, she wanted as much of him as she could get.
'Steve. . .I need you too.' Her admission was thick
with passion. She felt him flinch with the impact of the
sound.

His heat enveloped her; she was drawn into his
strength, the taut flex of muscles finding a soft bed in
her pliant flesh. His breath sawed through him, she
sobbed into his mouth, her tears on his hot flesh as he
pushed her closer to the brink of love, the silken sheath
of her body giving up its prize for the man who had
staked his claim as her lover from the first kiss they
had shared.

Cat felt as if her body was baked in golden fire,
dissolving every bone until she was liquid, flowing
between the sheets in a molten stream. Above her,
containing her, holding her earthbound shape, her
lover harnessed her beauty, tamed the wild gypsy
darkness and brought her safely back from a realm of
erotic insanity to the languor of exhaustion.

Cat lay in stunned silence, Steve's powerful chest
heaving against her soft, sensitive breasts, his breath
thunderous in her ear. He moved, taking her into the
shelter of his arms and stroking her soothingly as if she
needed to be comforted. She felt safe and cherished,
his lovemaking convincing her they had something

special. Lust, she concluded, couldn't give such a sense of well-being. . .such a sense of things being right.

'I could say I'm sorry,' he offered huskily, 'but I'd be lying.'

Cat had forgotten how they had got into bed. She gazed up at him, her gaze luminous with love. 'And you said Blood Star was dangerous.' Shyly, she smiled, turning to let her lips brush his chest.

'I may have left one or two bruises,' he murmured in a velvety tone that made her shiver deliciously. 'But no broken bones.'

'Are you sure?' Cat's eyes glittered mischievously.

'Almost sure. I guess I'd better check.'

It was a most thorough examination. Cat stretched luxuriously and submitted to his touch with a soft purr of satisfaction.

It was dark when Cat woke and looked dazedly around at her strange surroundings. Slowly, memory returned. The room was empty, Steve had gone. The bedside digital clock told her it was nine-thirty. Sitting up hurriedly, she felt her muscles protest and she held the sheet against her as the door opened and Sylvia Lucas entered, turning on the light and regarding the girl in bed with a recriminatory shake of her head.

'Silly girl. You should have contented yourself with Chas.'

'I. . . Where's Steve?'

'Steven? He's gone to reclaim his car from Cheetham's. He's not the type to get sentimental about exercising his appetite. He hated his father but they weren't all that different in that respect.'

'I don't understand. . .' Cat looked for her clothes, terribly embarrassed at being subjected to Sylvia Lucas's appraisal.

'I suppose I can tell you. We're both wrapped up in the same tragic comedy; you're almost like family.' Casually, she passed Cat her neatly stacked clothes and began a monologue.

'I left Ranleigh because I was pregnant.' Her wintry smile acknowledged the shock on Cat's face. 'Your mother was too dreamy to put two and two together. Your father, however, was more practical. He always carried out Ranleigh's dirty work for him. I was shipped off to America like a criminal. Edward Ranleigh never recognised my son, even when he came over here when he was eighteen. Your father and a few others threw him off the estate, giving him a good hiding for his audacity. They thought he was after the family money, when really he was just young, out to find out where he belonged.' She sighed. 'Steven swore he'd make so much money he'd buy Ranleigh from under Edward's feet and spit in his eye in the bargain. Farrells he would grind into the dust. When Thomas died, I thought Edward might try to heal the breach but there was nothing. When the estate came on to the market, the past rose up again and all Steven had to vent his anger on was you.'

Cat paled a deathly shade of white.

'You love him, don't you?'

She was too stunned to deny it, her eyes riveting on the bitter recognition in the older woman's gaze.

'I loved Edward Ranleigh. It did nothing to soften him. I'd like to think my son wouldn't wreak his revenge to the letter, but if he didn't protect you when you made love, then it's all rather prophetic, isn't it?'

Cat felt her skin goose-pimple with cold, shock gnawing at the satiation of her senses. Steve, Edward Ranleigh's son! Reclaiming his birthright and settling old scores with ruthless precision. How he must have

sneered at her talk of tradition. The traditions that
bound him to Ranleigh were those of hatred and
vengence. He had told her time distorted things and he
had personally felt the truth of those words. He had
had to buy his inheritance. No wonder he had been
furious when Chas had drawn up a contract that
benefited Farrells. Making her the instrument of
Farrells' demise was taking his pound of flesh from her
blood and bones.

'Get dressed and go home.' Sylvia Lucas got to her
feet. 'Times have changed. You can fight back.
Reclaim you pride. It took me ten years—I think the
modern woman should do a little better.'

Cat watched her leave and then hurried into action.
Tears slid down her cheeks. She had been right to
think there was some special ingredient to their lovemaking, but it hadn't been love! Steve had his final
moment of triumph, and hadn't he enjoyed it!

Steve Lucas was adept at turning her world into
ruins. She wouldn't give him the satisfaction of recri-
mination. This modern woman was going to do a lot
better!

CHAPTER NINE

CAT awoke the next morning in a mood of bleak despair. She couldn't take Steve Lucas's money. It would give him endless opportunities to interfere in her life, give him a rock-solid excuse to pursue an affair, exploiting her need of him.

Making the decision to refuse to be involved in any investment Steve Lucas made with Cheetham's, she tussled with the knowledge that Colonel Cheetham was unlikely to get the cash injection he was after. The threat of Farrells arising from the grave would be gone, however, and the Colonel could proceed with his business unchallenged by competition on his doorstep.

It was only courtesy to explain to Ronald Cheetham that she was backing out, and she made that her first task of the day. Surprisingly enough, the Colonel was reluctant to let her go.

'It was Penny causing mischief yesterday. Starter pistol,' he informed her, looking mortified. 'Gave her a good telling off, I can tell you. She's gone to London for a few days. Pulls a trick like that again, it's the end of her allowance.'

'I did rub her nose in it a bit.' Cat liked Colonel Cheetham and could see that he was upset about the incident.

'You're a good girl.' He patted her arm. 'And talented on a horse. How about if we put the deal on ice, as our American friend would say? If you ride Blood Star in the Maurier Cup and win, we could still do business with or without Steve Lucas.'

Cat was startled by the idea. But then it made perfect common sense. Her collateral would be high if she did well in the Maurier Cup. She would be an asset to Cheethams in her own right, rather than a package deal thrown in with Steve Lucas's money.

'If you're sure.' She kissed the Colonel's cheek, and he chuckled, giving her a hug.

'I'm sure. You're the only one that manages to make Blood Star look worth the money I paid for him. Do well in the cup and we're both winners.'

That morning, Cat managed to complete the practice circuit. The stallion tossed his head and pulled a little but showed none of the fiery temperament of the day before.

Her next call was Felicity Barnhurst's. She was housing Shannon along with her own two horses, Firelight and Butterfly. She had insisted on putting up the bay thoroughbred to make amends for embarrassing Cat with her thoughtless gossip.

She had heard about Penny's prank and was avid. Cat played down the incident for Colonel Cheetham's sake.

'How's Shannon doing?'

'Oh, he's settled in fairly well. A bit off his feed yesterday but he's eating his head off today, so nothing to worry about.'

Cat was relieved. She had felt guilty about spending time with Blood Star when her own horse needed exercise. She tacked-up and exercised the bay, enjoying the morning ride, the pale blue sky and ripe gold of the countryside doing something to chase away the misery that had enveloped her that morning.

She was using a hoof-pick to clean the underpart of Shannon's hoof when she heard someone enter the stable.

'I'd love a cup of coffee if you're making one,' she muttered, concentrating hard on a stubborn piece of mud, under the impression she was talking to Felicity.

Steve Lucas regarded her critically. Wearing beige jodhpurs and a matching patterned jumper, black hair tied back in a plait, she looked like a heroine out of a girls' magazine rather than the full-blooded woman he knew her to be.

'You don't stay around long enough for coffee,' he commented with dry sarcasm, watching her flinch as she recognised his voice. 'Why did you leave last night? I was only gone an hour.'

Rosy-cheeked, she continued with her task, not able to bring herself to look at him. His voice brought back memories of the things he had whispered to her in the heat of passion. She'd avoided thinking about him all morning. It hit her hard, how easily he could trigger her responses.

'Well?' He sounded impatient.

'Do we have to have a post-mortem? It's done. Over. What was I supposed to do, applaud?' Releasing Shannon's heel, she forced herself to meet his eyes, her own lit with tension.

Frowning, Steve's eyes flickered to the horse as it moved, made restless by the explosive atmosphere.

'Over?' he latched on to the word, his gaze stormy. 'What's that supposed to mean? Nothing's over, sweetheart, until I say it is.' Grabbing her arm, he hauled her back as she made a move to continue Shannon's grooming. 'Forget the horse! What is it with you?' His voice was rough and uneven. 'Last night you——'

'I don't want to talk about it!' She vigorously tried to free herself from his hold. 'Get—off—me.'

Convinced by the determination in her face, he let

go and regarded her as if she was the most aggravating creature he had ever come across.

'Are you upset because I left you? You were sleeping. . . I had some important files in the car I needed for this morning.' Raking his fingers through his hair, his eyes showed how little he liked explaining himself. 'I didn't like returning to find you gone, either. . . You've made your point. It was a lousy thing to do and I'm sorry.'

He was very good, Cat congratulated him with silent bitterness. If his own mother hadn't confirmed his treachery, she would have been almost convinced that he meant it.

'I'm really not interested,' she replied with cool hauteur. 'If you don't mind, I've got work to do.'

'But I do mind.' He placed himself in her path. 'So what does it take to make you easily bedded? The cottage? Is that the idea? Give me a taste and make me beg?' He vibrated with masculine aggression. 'Let's work out an instalment plan. I'm willing to be practical.'

Knowing he was trying to blast her out of her hostile resistance and into more emotional territory, she kept a hold on her temper.

'I'm sure you are.' She regarded him with dislike. 'Last night I had to get away to think. I'm not going to become any more deeply involved with a man who treats people like commodities. You have to be in control, don't you, Steve, have to have the whip hand?' She shook her head, disbelief darkening her eyes to the colour of jet. 'That's why you used your own money to invest at Cheetham's, so you could blackmail me into doing what you wanted, when you wanted. Well, I'm pleased to inform you I've told Colonel Cheetham I want no part of any investment you wish to make in his business. What you choose to do about the cottage. . .' She gave a helpless shrug. 'It will be difficult. But we'll survive.'

'Brave words.' He regarded her with hooded eyes, his mouth in a stubborn line. 'Let's see how long it takes you to regret them.' Cat maintained her ground as he came close to her, his breath warm on her face as he spoke. 'And you will regret them, Catherine, be sure of that.'

The stable reverberated with echoes of menace long after he had left. Cat was rigid with tension, her hard-fought-for bravery deserting her completely. She was back at the beginning. Primrose Cottage was still part of Lucas-Brett's investment and her family's future, once again, hung in the balance.

Three days later, a man in a business suit presented himself at the door of Primrose Cottage, showing a letter from the owners of Ranleigh giving him permission to value the cottage. Cat showed him around in tight-lipped silence. He was only doing his job. She knew who lay behind the valuation and why.

Chas visited with an invitation to the 'house-warming'. In reality it was a sneak preview for various invited notables to encourage a membership rush at Ranleigh as soon as the golf-course opened. Jessica Farrell accepted the invitation for the family and Cat was torn between dreaming up a good excuse and alternatively braving it out to show Steve she was capable of dismissing him from her life without regret.

The morning before the party at Ranleigh, a white envelope came through the door, addressed to Cat. Inside was a valuation of Primrose Cottage, the price astronomical and in the words of the valuer 'consistent with the value to be expected of a property within the grounds of such a magnificent estate, now to be used as an exclusive leisure park.' The fact that it was addressed to her and not her mother proved that it was Steve Lucas who had targeted her as the recipient of the information.

Half an hour later, the phone rang. Cat picked it up and bit her lip as she heard the voice at the other end of the line.

'What do you want?' She kept her tone neutral, knowing that her mother was nearby arranging some flowers in a vase.

'You.' The word was softly spoken but sent Cat's hormones into overdrive.

'I'm afraid I'm not available. I'm sure if you ring around you'll find someone willing to take up your business.' As she ground the receiver back into its cradle, a militant light shone in Cat's dark eyes.

That night she cast off the 'demure miss' image that had failed her at Cheetham's in favour of a strapless black cocktail dress, with a black sequinned bodice and a layered skirt. It had been bought for her eighteenth birthday party, the day when she officially took over the business matters of the family and fancied herself as a grown woman rather than a burdened teenager.

Unless persuaded otherwise, her hair waved naturally. Giving the ebony locks their freedom, she was startled at the exotic creature returning her gaze in the mirror. She looked positively feline. Snatching her gaze away, she was haunted by the knowledge that the woman made the dress, not the other way around. Tonight she needed all the protective armour she could get. If Steve was going to romance Serena Hamilton, Cat was going to remind him of exactly what money couldn't buy!

That night, as the Farrells approached the manor

house on foot, it seemed as if Ranleigh had come alive.
Light glittered from the windows and the courtyard
was full of expensive machinery. Jamie counted four
Rolls-Royces and a litter of Mercedes and Porsches.

Ranleigh's restaurant had been divided into two.
Tables covered in white damask, decorated with
flowers and flickering candles, occupied one half of the
room, the other was cordoned off for dancing.

Waiters wove in and out of the assembled throng,
champagne and sherry being served in abundance. An
open bar provided spirits for anyone who preferred
something stronger.

Chas intercepted the Farrells, winking at Cat, who
smiled at him with warmth. He was all charm; his
erstwhile fiancée had yet to make an appearance.

'You look gorgeous,' he complimented her. 'Let me
introduce you to my family.'

The Lucases *en masse* were impressive. Steve stood
slightly to one side in conversation with an elderly man,
whose well groomed grey hair and pale eyes gave an
urbane grace to a shrewd intellect. Frank Lucas, she
guessed as the introductions took place. There was
nothing subservient in Steve's manner to the older
man, although respect was evident on both sides.

Cat politely shook hands in turn, her eyes held by
Frank Lucas as he retained possession of her fingers
for a few seconds so that she couldn't move on.

'So you're Catherine? Steve tells me you're good
enough to ride in a rodeo. Is he exaggerating about
this monstrous stallion?'

She smiled cautiously. Frank Lucas had obviously
heard about her exploits on Blood Star. Aware of the
leisurely inspection she was being subjected to, her
eyes flickered sideways to duel with Steve's.

'I don't think Steve likes horses very much. Blood

Star is high-spirited but manageable once he gives his trust. Colonel Cheetham, who owns the horse, has entered him for the Maurier Cup.'

'Do you intend to ride him?'

'Yes. I think we stand a good chance.'

Cat heard the indrawn hiss of Steve's breath, her eyes drawn to the furious glitter in his.

Frank Lucas heard too and turned to view his protégé with a glint of humour. 'A determined young lady.'

'Foolhardy comes to mind.' A silent war was being waged, Cat's eyes telling him to go to hell.

'I'll make you eat your words,' she responded lightly before moving on to greet Chas's parents.

Gloria and Mitch Lucas weren't very forthcoming and she gathered from their warmth when Serena appeared, in a claret, figure-hugging dress, that they had decided ideas about their son's future that didn't include a penniless upstart like Cat Farrell.

'Steve, you're not to talk business all night,' Serena pouted. Her eyes moved to Cat, over-bright and a little desperate. 'Tell him he mustn't, Catherine. I'm sure he'd take notice of you.'

Cat didn't know quite what to make of that. Her uncertainty brought a gleam of sardonic humour to Steve's gaze.

'Don't be taken in by appearances, Serena. Catherine is more interested in slugging it out with a rogue stallion. We mere males are beneath her notice. A terrible pity——' he all but stripped her with his gaze '—but unfortunately true.'

Cat's chin lifted, her eyes obsidian, pride stamped on her features. Her light, tinkling laugh made their conversation flirtatious rather than the outright warfare that it most certainly was.

'Steve. . .' The husky note in her voice held a hint of intimacy, making Serena look uncomfortable, as she realised what she had started. 'You can't possibly be jealous of a horse. I'm sure there are plenty of women who would be only too eager to distract you from your work.' Her voice trailed off, deliberately refusing the reassurance that she would be in their number.

Eyes of heated azure baked her alive. He had the ability to isolate her from every other soul in the room and slash at her defences.

'Some women,' he affirmed smokily, 'don't even have to try.'

He cruised to victory, a wave of heat licking from Cat's toes to surge up her body, her lashes sweeping down to avoid that visual seduction that penetrated deep into her flesh.

'Let's mingle.' Chas's voice had a suffocated tone to it and Cat fell in with his plans with relief. Her body cooled slowly as they distanced themselves from the reception party and were absorbed on to the dance-floor.

'I think you just upped my chances with Serena.' Chas directed a wicked smile at her confusion. 'No one witnessing that little scene would call you just good friends. He must be losing his cool to throw in his hand just like that.'

Cat viewed him with despair. 'Steve won't lose unless he wants to.' She spoke with absolute conviction and watched him pale, impressed by her words.

She felt sorry for him, sorry for Serena and sorry for herself. Steve Lucas was a driven man, willing to damage three lives to carve an empire that would outshine the father who had never acknowledged him. He deserved a loveless marriage! She should be glad Sylvia Lucas had allowed her to escape with her pride intact. If only she could numb the pain. She felt as if someone had knifed her between the ribs.

Steve Lucas stood on the edge of the crowd, his head lifted, like an animal scenting its prey. His eyes narrowed, his mouth firming ominously when Chas spontaneously hugged Cat.

'Don't let him see.' Chas spoke close to her ear. 'He's watching every move you make.'

Cat never quite lost her awareness of Steve's threatening presence. She stayed on the dance-floor, feeling safer there, surrounded by her friends and manufacturing a brittle gaiety that masked her inner distress. In normal circumstances she liked dancing, but that night the rhythmic sway of her hips to the music was automatic, her mind definitely elsewhere.

Serena had joined them and was jiving with Henry Winterton. Her attempted vivacity was something Cat recognised. She wondered which of the Lucas men was fuelling Serena.

The music slowed down and Chas took her into his arms, a mischievous grin asking for her compliance.

'Is your plan working?' she asked reprovingly. 'I presume you're trying to make Serena miserable?'

'Oh, I think she's miserable, but then Steve's been about as forthcoming as a rock all evening. Oh-oh, the rock moveth,' he murmured in mock biblical fashion.

Cat stiffened but she needn't have worried. Steve smiled at Serena and cut in on Henry Winterton. The young woman snuggled into him, creating a well of black jealousy to poison Cat's reason. Chas took advantage of her devastation to whirl her out on to the terrace, using the startled lift of her face to his to press his lips against her mouth.

The next few seconds were indelibly printed on Cat's memory. One minute Chas was kissing her surprised lips, the next he was descending to the floor with a small crowd of interested observers turning towards the French windows.

Her wrist was grasped in Steve's punishing grip. Serena was bending to see to Chas, who was nursing his jaw. Cat suffered the humiliation of being hauled off into the shrubbery in full view of several of the county's biggest gossips.

'How dare you?' She pulled away as soon as they passed out of sight, into the stillness of Ranleigh's landscaped gardens. 'How dare you make a scene like that?'

'I dare,' he breathed through clenched teeth. Anger fused his bones into a mask of pure fury. 'What's the matter, Catherine? Are you feeling frustrated? If you want your blood cooling, you come to me! I didn't give you a taste for sex to see you flaunt yourself in front of every available male in the room.'

She visibly shook with temper but reined it in with supreme effort. 'Don't talk to me as if I owe you anything,' she scorned him. 'What I have a taste for——' her eyes clashed with his as she copied his crude expression '—is love, and you didn't give me that! You couldn't, you wouldn't know how!'

'If you want me to love you, you have a funny way of showing it,' he snarled, catching and holding her as she attempted to move past him.

Cat felt his fingers dig into her upper arms, bruising the soft flesh. His eyes were a furious blend of anger and frustration and she felt a moment of satisfaction that she could drive him to that.

'Wasn't it you who told me not to waste my time on lost causes?' she retaliated coldly, trying to shrug him off. 'You shouldn't have hit Chas. How will that look to Lee Hamilton?'

'Kissing you didn't do much for Chas's cause. He deserved what he got for playing with Serena's emotions.'

'I don't think your white knight act is going to wash.' Her eyes showed the pain he was inflicting, but he was too inflamed to notice.

'No? People believe what they want to believe.' Something heated in those light eyes, so vivid against the copper tan of his skin. Hard purpose underscored his taunting words, his anger becoming more subtle, channelled into the hot ache of wanting. 'If I wanted a rich wife, the circles I move in are dripping with women with money.'

His eyes dropped to the pale skin his grip had reddened. His fingers began an insidious massage, hardly moving at first, then flexing and sensually stroking over her throbbing flesh. Molten rivers of heat ran along her bones as his gaze took in the sooty dark eyes that rejected and beckoned him at the same time. His lean fingers moved to the back of her neck in a sinuous movement, his eyes hypnotic in their threat.

'You're sending me messages I don't understand. Name your price and I might leave Chas in one piece.'

'I don't want your rotten money!' She caught her breath as his fingers slid down the indentation of her spine to its base, lingering there to create tiny explosions of desire.

'Money isn't the only means of barter.' His gaze was unrelentingly sexual, and Cat's breath caught in her throat as he mesmerised her with sinful, sensual promises that tortured her flesh.

'I'm not some young boy who's going to spill his heart out after one tumble between the sheets. Besides anything else——' his head bent nearer, stirring the small dark hairs at her temple '—I didn't have the breath. . .'

Cat stirred at his words, her beautiful face alight with challenge as she suffered the burning need in his. Tilting her head back, her lips were inches from his, trembling slightly at the proximity.

'So how long does it take, Steve? Weeks? Months? If I let you take me back to bed, will your heart ever soften enough to want more than just sex?'

'Why do I get the feeling that isn't a genuine question?' Steve regarded her with frightening perception. 'What is it that's firing you up like this? I know I forced things between us, but we both know you were willing. I don't think I hurt you, any more than I could help. . .' His gaze interrogated her, witnessing the fiery blush that discussing such intimacies brought to her cheeks. 'You can talk to me about it, Catherine. I know the first time must be difficult for a woman. . . and I guess at the moment you don't feel like confiding in any of your friends.'

Cat felt bitter humour curdle in her throat. He thought her rejection came from the shock of initiation into womanhood. He was even willing to counsel her through the process. What a thoughtful lover, she derided silently.

'Do you really want to know?' she asked with deceptive softness. 'Do you want to know why I will never let you use me again——?'

'Catherine!' he bit out her name in protest.

'You laid down the terms of our relationship,' she pointed out, her breath disintegrating as his fingers surged up to circle her throat. 'You showed a surprising degree of honesty about that. Clever of you to cover up your real motives for changing the face of Ranleigh. If I'd known what sort of man I was dealing with I would never have parted with one square inch of the land Farrells was built on.'

'Wouldn't you, darling?' His thumbs massaged her throat with the lightness of a butterfly's wing. He watched her with a waiting calm. 'Why not?'

'You know perfectly well,' she whispered, aware of the threat he embodied and yet not able to stop herself. She was sick of the lies. Sick of the subterfuge. 'I wouldn't have let you crush what my family built up under your heel. I hope you gained satisfaction from that because you won't get any more from me.'

'But I want more from you.' His breath feathered her lips. 'I want you breathless. I want your hair running like black silk over my pillow. I want your lips to tease me to hell and back and your thighs to give me heaven——'

'Shut up!' She denied the fever he was raising in her blood. 'Oh, please stop, Steve, I——'

'Can't stand it,' he groaned against her lips. 'Neither can I. I don't know why we're fighting but I sure as hell know how to stop it.'

Cat panicked as he opened his mouth over hers, knowing how easily he could arouse her. Her lips were crushed and dominated as he shamelessly exploited her desire to melt weakly against him. She was being sucked down into a whirlpool of black swirling emotion where only satiation of her senses remained a coherent demand.

Somewhere in those treacherous depths, Sylvia Lucas's cold, bitter face swam up to meet her and she felt a surge of rebellion well up inside her.

Wrenching her mouth from his, she slapped his face and tore herself out of his arms as the element of surprise gave her a momentary advantage. How devious he was to try and humiliate her further. To make her ache for his possession when she was in full possession of the facts made his victory complete.

'Is this part of your revenge too?' she demanded emotionally. Her gypsy darkness held a passionate ferocity, her black hair with those rebellious waves writhing over her shoulders, her breasts heaving against the black sequinned bodice of her dress. 'Because of the past, you intend to throw my family off the estate and shame me in front of everyone I know and respect. Will that make you happy, Steve? Will destroying me satisfy you?'

He froze, his face immobile. A sudden flash of awareness sharpened his features. 'What are you talking about? Who's been talking to you?'

'Do you deny you're Edward Ranleigh's son? That you swore you'd get even for the way he treated you? You promised to see Farrells driven into the dust and you've succeeded, haven't you? You even made me preside over its carcass.'

Steve Lucas regarded her with the stillness of the jungle cat before it pounced. 'You think I convinced Lucas-Brett to buy the estate to make those in it suffer? My father and yours are both dead, Catherine. Do you really believe my pride would be satisfied taking revenge on a nineteen-year-old girl?'

His scathing tone weakened her momentarily, doubt flickering in her gaze and then dying.

'Don't try and deny it. You've destroyed Ranleigh! There's not one single family left living on the estate. You've got rid of them all because they obeyed Edward Ranleigh and——'

'Beat me up for daring to embarrass the lord of the manor with my existence?' He laughed humourlessly. 'You have a lurid sense of revenge.'

'Don't laugh at me.' She was incensed. 'You resent this place. You couldn't have it, so you wanted to spoil it for everyone else. I must have been your finest hour. . . You've taken everything I had, even my dreams, and manufactured them in your image.'

'Only because they were unrealistic,' Steve cut into her angry words with freezing logic. 'You can't live in a fairy-tale, Catherine——'

'Where do you want me to live? Thanks to your company, my family will have to leave Ranleigh too.' Her small face was alive with an inner flame, aware of the visible hardening of his features as her words spilled hotly between them. 'I hope you'll feel honour satisfied when we move out. I suppose if you've made me pregnant, it will make revenge taste sweet. I don't think your mother will relish your success! To find out her son is as cruel and ruthless as his father strikes me as a rather bitter harvest.'

Steve Lucas approached her slowly. His control was on a knife edge—she could read it in the flare of his nostrils and the stiff breadth of his shoulders.

'No one speaks to me like that.' His finger was like ice as it slid against her jaw, cold fury leaping from his eyes. 'I don't know where you picked up this baggage of half-truths you're carrying around, but I promise you, I didn't take your sweet little body to bring a child into the world that I would callously reject. Neither would I make a woman pregnant who has barely left childhood and finds the demands of being an adult so patently difficult to deal with!' Grasping her chin, he jerked her head back so that she was forced to meet his eyes. 'I took care of you when we made love. And I'll keep taking care of you until I know you're safe. Now get out of my sight before I forget my good intentions and strangle you with my bare hands. I need very little temptation.'

Cat didn't need telling twice. She fled.

CHAPTER TEN

IT WASN'T until the next day that Cat discovered what being taken care of meant. She arrived at Cheetham's at nine just to see Blood Star disappearing in a horse-box.

'What's going on?' she asked one of the stable lads.

'He kicked Mickey yesterday. The boss has sold him. Lucky to get a good price too—that horse is a menace.'

Ronald Cheetham was sympathetic but firm. 'I'm sorry, Catherine. The horse was costing me money. I'll have Mickey sick for a couple of months. Blood Star broke his arm. I know he was good for you but I couldn't turn down the offer I got for him. After he bolted, no one local would bid for him, and with Mickey it was the last straw.'

Cat felt as if she was bedevilled by catastrophe. Her life over the last month had raged from despair to hope and back again with such rapidity that she felt dizzy.

'Who bought him?' she asked as an afterthought, to see Cheetham shift uncomfortably.

'I couldn't say for certain. There was a middle-man. But the banker's draft was in dollars.'

Cat's head lifted, her pale face suffusing with colour. Why would some unknown American buy Blood Star? It had to be Steve. He was determined she wouldn't ride the stallion. When she disobeyed his wishes, he simply bought the horse from under her.

She made a detour to Ranleigh on her way home. Her intention to confront Steve with his treachery over Blood Star faltered as she entered the hallway and spied her mother and Jamie sitting in one of the reception rooms accompanied by their solicitor Peter Bainbridge.

'Ah, Catherine.' The solicitor beckoned her. 'Come in. We were waiting for you.'

Cat was bewildered. How could they know she'd be on her way to Ranleigh? Moving into the room, her question was answered. It didn't take much intuition on Steve's part to know she would come to the manor after her visit to Cheethams. Her adversary was standing by the window and Frank Lucas was sitting in one of the studded leather armchairs, all apparently gathered for some sort of meeting.

'Maybe now we can begin.' Steve accurately read the seethe of emotions Cat was barely containing, his knowing look inflaming her further. 'Coffee?' he offered politely, enjoying the frustrated glitter in her eyes. Cat had no intention of giving another public performance and he knew it.

'No, thank you.' She frowned questioningly. 'Is something wrong?'

'No, no,' her mother smiled a little anxiously. 'Steven was just explaining the problems involved in resiting Farrells. It seems it's going to cause all sorts of difficulties and. . .well, Lucas-Brett are willing to offer us the cottage in settlement of the contract.' She looked up at Peter Bainbridge, who nodded with a satisfied air. All eyes turned to Cat. Frank Lucas was watching her with keen interest, his fingers steepled, brushing lightly against his lips.

It had been the last thing she had expected. Lucas-Brett were willing to hand over the cottage, just like that! She knew by the hard glint in Steve's eyes that he was mocking her heated accusations of the night before. Just what trick had he up his sleeve now? Cat dragged her gaze from Steve to question Frank Lucas.

'This new offer. . .it is on behalf of your company, Mr Lucas? Lucas-Brett wouldn't be acting as an agent for any other party?'

Frank Lucas smiled faintly. 'No, my dear. The cottage is being offered in settlement by Lucas-Brett. No other party is involved.'

'I don't quite understand. . .' Peter Bainbridge looked perplexed.

'You don't need to.' Steve was abrupt, temper flaring in his eyes. 'I'm sure you would like to time to discuss the matter. Frank. . .' He waited for the older man to join him. Cat waylaid him at the door, deliberately blocking his path.

'Yes?' His voice questioned her in grating undertone. 'What can I do for you?' Eyes as cool as arctic waters washed over her.

'There's something I wish to discuss with you. Have you got a moment?' It was a restrained request, to put it mildly.

'I'm busy.' He glanced at his watch. 'Can't it wait?'

'No.' She was resolute,

'I'll talk to the Paris office.' Frank Lucas rested a hand lightly on the younger man's shoulder. 'You should always have time for beautiful young ladies.'

Steve Lucas gave his mentor a rather jaundiced look but acquiesced, inviting Cat to precede him into his office with a curt nod of his head.

'Just what are you up to now?' she demanded furiously as soon as the office door had closed behind him. 'This is all very sudden. You were planning to evict me two weeks ago!'

'Was I?' he drawled sarcastically. 'You're always so

sure you know my motives. It makes me feel practically transparent.'

Cat was thrown into confusion by his tone. He sounded as if his patience was running thin.

'You've bought Blood Star,' she accused bitterly. 'Or are you going to deny that too? How can you expect me to take this sudden change of heart by Lucas-Brett at face value when you manipulate my life in any way you can? You can't bear not getting your own way, can you? If Steve Lucas can't win the game, he moves the goalposts.'

'Is that what you came to say?' he enquired with mocking patience. 'That I've offended some sacred code of fairness by stopping you riding a homicidal horse.'

'Blood Star is——'

'Blood Star is temperamental verging on vicious.' He circled his desk, going to the other side and picking up some stray items of post. Blue eyes assaulted her with a brief searing criticism before returning to scan a letter dismissively. 'You'd see that yourself if you weren't so busy trying to get one over on me.'

'My choice of horse has got nothing to do with you! Only a supreme egotist would think so!' Leaning forward, she tore the letter out of his hand, demanding his attention. 'You can't bear the thought that I might be able to succeed without you, can you?'

Bearing his weight on his forearms, he came within inches of her face, his gaze alive with treacherous undercurrents.

'I can't bear the thought of you ending up in hospital! I have plans for your body that don't involve it being encased in plaster.'

She moved back in alarm at his close proximity, Steve's eyes narrowing at her reaction.

'You could have a decent horse. I'm still willing to put money into Cheetham's. The only one creating obstacles to your future is you.'

'I've seen the way you operate.' She glanced back at him with disdain. 'To say I'm not impressed is an understatement.'

His sardonic laughter made her eyes flare. He had a way of making her sound very naïve and unworldly.

'You haven't a clue how I operate.' Coming around the side of the desk, he shoved his hands in his pockets and observed her with his head tilted slightly to one side. 'By the way, Chas and Serena have made up their differences. They plan to get married in Gretna Green. Lee Hamilton was impressed by Chas handling this deal. Frank touched up the school report.'

'Many commiserations. Still, as you say, it shouldn't take you long to find another heiress. Better luck next time.'

Steve ignored that. 'He said he kissed you to make Serena jealous.'

Cat smiled mockingly. 'And Serena made eyes at you to have the same effect on Chas. That must be a blow to the ego.'

'They sound like two confused people.'

Cat looked at him, aware of some unspoken message but too angry to interpret it. She turned the door-handle. 'I don't suppose they'll be the first or last. I'm riding Shannon in the Maurier Cup. I trust you have no objection to that.' Her sarcasm would have cut a less assured individual to shreds.

'None at all. I remember you telling me once that he had great heart. You seemed to think that was worth a lot before I expressed my doubts about the stallion.'

He knew just what buttons to press. With a fierce look, Cat thrust the door open and slammed it behind her. How dare he presume to question her loyalties? It was because of him that she had to try to make a living out of her prowess as a rider. Without Farrells she was just another girl mad about horses. That wouldn't pay the bills and help Jamie out at university. Resolve hardened within her. She was going to concentrate all her energy on the show-jumping event ahead of her. She would show him just how little she needed his arrogant, authoritative intrusion into her life!

The acceptance of Primrose Cottage as the final settlement of the deal with Lucas-Brett was agreed that day. Despite Cat's misgivings over Steve's motives, Cat couldn't deny her mother the security of knowing her home and future were safe.

'Well, I think that draws everything to a satisfying conclusion.' Frank Lucas signed for Lucas-Brett, his pale eyes shrewd as they briefly met Cat's.

One of the staff had entered with a tray containing champagne and a number of glasses. The others in the room had moved to anticipate the celebration.

'Steve will be able to concentrate his energies elsewhere. This has been difficult for him,' the elderly man confided quietly. 'He did specifically ask not to develop this project, in line with his abstention vote on the purchase. Unfortunately, as Lucas-Brett's chief negotiator, he had little choice but to get Chas out of a mess.'

Cat regarded the silver-haired president of Lucas-Brett with a sudden intensity of interest. She was wary, knowing from the few times she had seen the two Lucas men together that they had an intuitive understanding of the other.

'Did he ask you to tell me that?' she asked, bitterness making her doubt the truth of what had been said.

'Steve?' Frank Lucas's brief laughter was as dry as old parchment. 'I thought you knew him better than that, my dear.'

Jamie approached with a glass in each hand, breaking into the exchange. Frank Lucas took one, lifting it and proposed a well polished toast to the future.

Cat had a lot to think about during the days that were left to the staging of the Maurier Cup. She practised daily at Cheetham's, having come to a satisfactory arrangement with the Colonel. It took a lot to admit, but the Farrells' prospects were far more solidly based now they owned their own home and had part ownership in a prosperous modern stables.

The Lucases decamped in stages. Chas and Serena opted for their romantic elopement and Frank, Sylvia Lucas and Lee Hamilton returned to the States to arrange a suitable reception for the newly married couple upon their return home.

Only Steve remained to see Ranleigh opening its doors to membership and, Cat knew, it wouldn't be long before business drew him elsewhere.

When the day of the Maurier Cup dawned, Cat went through the motions of preparation. She felt miserable. The lowering skies seemed to echo her mood. She missed Steve. No, that wasn't quite right, she missed their intimacy, their fights, those blue eyes teasing her. When their paths had crossed he was back in professional mode.

Cat had desperately wanted to set things straight with him. She'd had time to think. Giving Primrose Cottage to the Farrells had been proof positive that Steve wasn't driven by revenge in his dealings with her family. Knowing he was behind the settlement, she had taken the offer made by Lucas-Brett as some complex subterfuge, refusing to see Steve as anything else but

an arch manipulator. Frank Lucas's assurance that
Steve hadn't wanted anything to do with the project
also weighed heavily on her mind. She had wanted to
apologise but the moment never seemed right.

Cat recalled the time he had come to Cheetham's to
watch her practise. She had completed the circuit, to
see him leaning against the fence watching her. Dressed
in faded denims and a white shirt, she had moved
quickly to cover up her traitorous response.

Dropping the reins, she had played the clown. 'Look,
no hands.'

'Shannon wouldn't hurt a hair on your head,' he'd
replied enigmatically. 'How's it going?'

'Slow but sure.' Dismounting, she had unfastened
her chin-strap and stripped off the gloves she used for
riding. 'Have you come to see the Colonel?'

Ignoring the question, he let cool blue eyes slide
over her. 'You look as if you've lost weight. Is that
necessary for the competition?'

Cat was immediately on the defensive. It was true,
she had lost weight, but it had nothing to do with the
show-jumping event ahead.

'I must be pining.' She had darted him an impudent
look. 'Is that what you wanted to hear?'

Steve had regarded her with calculated patience.
'Pining for what?'

'Success,' she'd returned brightly, hating his derisive
smile and wishing she hadn't confronted him and had
made her peace instead. The longer she left it, the
more it played on her mind.

A horse coming up close by made Shannon snort and
shift uncomfortably and brought her back to the present. Penny Cheetham was riding Mr Martin in the
competition, an expensive roan. She viewed Shannon
with faint disdain.

'Poor Cinders. Back on that hack. Pity your lover thought you weren't competent to ride Blood Star. You might have stood a chance.'

Cat looked past her, at the fine drizzle shrouding the arena. 'I would have had to pull Blood Star out; he didn't favour soft turf.'

Penelope whirled around with an audible, 'Damn!' Stalking off, she went to confer with her father.

The misty drizzle continued. Cat was in the last three to jump. So far there was one clear round and the rest of the field all had penalty points. Mighty Jack, ridden by Jeff Barstow, had the only clear round by the time it got to Cat's turn. She rode Shannon into the ring, while the commentator told the spectators of her past successes.

The first three fences flew past in a swift succession, Shannon carefully negotiating the coloured bar fences. She could hear the claps and cheers, feel Shannon snorting and breathing hard as he lined up for the water. Horse and rider flew through the air, shrouded in small droplets of water from the sky, Shannon determined to avoid the watery shallows and move on to the next jump. The wall loomed and Shannon corrected himself with perfect timing. It was like a dream; they had never been more in tune. When she cleared the last fence and Shannon proudly subsided into a trot, she was laughing with disbelief.

She had the second clear round with only two to go. Patting Shannon's neck, she dismounted, letting Trevor see to Shannon while she went to the edge of the enclosure to watch.

'Is this what you want to do for the rest of your life? Push a stubborn animal over some God-forsaken swamp in the rain?' The soft drawl made her glance sharply to her left.

'Steve! What are you doing here?' Shockwaves danced from her scalp to her toes.

He shrugged casually. 'Trying to understand the fascination. One down, one to go,' he murmured, smiling to himself as she glanced at the arena with slow comprehension. 'Looks as if you're in the prize money whatever happens.'

So it seemed. The final horse had a refusal at the wall and it was between Mighty Jack and Shannon for first prize.

'Good luck.' He brushed a mud splash from her cheek and flipped the peak of her riding hat.

His touch disturbed her effortlessly. Cat looked up into his face, the familiar tough mould of his features absorbing her until his eyebrow quirked and she tore her gaze away hurriedly. Heat crept under her skin and she was glad of the urgency of the competition, making remounting her horse necessary. Why had he come? Why did he torment her with these fleeting expressions of interest?

The course demanded her attention and she concentrated hard. The second round was down to time and she knew Mighty Jack was quicker. Jeff Barstow rode out, taking it carefully but aware that whatever target he set would be there to beat. Haste at the water cost him four faults but his time was very respectable considering the conditions.

Cat had no illusions. The only way to win was to get a clear round. If she tied on penalty points the other horse would take first prize.

Carefully she gathered up the reins and spoke quietly to Shannon. His ears pricked up and they were off.

The arena was unnervingly quiet. Shannon seemed to make a lot of noise, his powerful quarters working as he covered the distance between one fence and

another. The water flashed past her, the wall a blur
until she faced the final combination. She steadied
Shannon, felt her breath course hotly through her
body, then with muttered encouragement, her knees
urging him on, Shannon built speed and jumped. A
flashlight blinded Cat. She merely kept her position on
the horse, feeling Shannon leap for the second time
and hearing the crash as she hit the other side. Blinking
rapidly, she realised the crash was of hundreds of hands
beating together in celebration. The commentator was
excitedly claiming, 'A new star is born. Catherine
Farrell, winner of the Chalfont Cup, has today shown
us that she has an enduring talent. Well done, Cat!'

When she dismounted, Steve lifted her off her feet
and whirled her around, his blue eyes alive with
pleasure. Cat steadied herself, her hands on his
shoulders, aware of those gathering around them, not
in the least prepared to be kissed breathless as she was
allowed to touch the ground.

'What are you doing?' She blinked up at him,
confused, as the tall American announced there would
be an open bar at Ranleigh that night to honour her
victory.

'Celebrating your coming of age,' he replied, viewing
her bewildered expression with interest. His eyes
reminded her of summer skies, warm with the midday
sun. 'Your fairy-tale's real now, princess. Enjoy it.'

Something serious touched that light gaze and Cat's
eyes lingered before she was engulfed by family and
friends. Was that how he had seen her nostalgia for the
old days? A refusal to grow up—a refusal to leave her
childhood security and strike out for her place in the
future? Cat glanced back but he had gone, swallowed
up by the crowd.

She had to wait for the presentation ceremony at the

end of the day. That night, she would dress in all her finery and do the decent thing. She would give Steve his long-overdue apology. It would be difficult because she knew that, despite her misconceptions about him, nothing had changed between them. He still wanted a brief, emotionless affair. She would be all sorts of fool if she let her vulnerable heart sway her head and indulged the hunger in her body in a passionate goodbye.

Cat chose a clinging flame-coloured dress that drew attention to her womanly curves. Silver bracelets jangled at her wrists, her shoulders bare, the thinnest of straps supporting the stunning simplicity of the creation. She was determined to say goodbye in full warpaint!

'You look very nice, darling.' Jessica Farrell smiled benignly.

Jamie gave a wolf-whistle, his eyes dancing with devilment. 'Planning to slay some poor unsuspecting male?' he teased. 'Now who could that be?'

Jessica smiled approvingly. 'I think it was very nice of Steven to offer Ranleigh for your party. I think he has a soft spot for you, Catherine.'

Cat exchanged a glance with her brother. Steve Lucas might have dragged the younger members of the Farrell family into the real world but her mother was an incurable romantic.

Entering the manor, Cat walked through the door her brother held open for her, to enter the lounge that was to be the exclusive preserve of the golf club. There were already over twenty people present and the music was bearable but loud.

Steve detached himself from the end of the bar when he caught sight of her. He wore a lightweight suit with a black T-shirt underneath. Regarding her with devas-

tating intensity, he dismissed Jamie with a glance and
shackled her wrist with strong, determined fingers.

'What the hell have you got on?' He spoke in a low
impassioned tone. 'I think I preferred your Sunday
School outfit.'

Cat was astonished. The last thing she had expected
from Steve was a puritanical outburst about her state
of dress.

'It's perfectly reasonable.' She glanced down at her
body to see the jut of her breasts explicitly outlined,
her reaction to his closeness all too blatant.

Colour splashed her cheeks at his tight, 'Exactly,'
and she found herself enveloped in his jacket and
unceremoniously escorted from the room.

'Oh, no!' Cat dug her heels into the rich pile of the
hall carpet as he hauled her towards the stairs. 'I'm not
going up there, Steve!' She was outraged as he lifted
her off her feet and took the stairs two at a time.

'Yes, you are,' he muttered. 'Unless you want this
conversation in front of your friends, which I very
much doubt.'

Cat didn't hide her resentment, struggling all the
way. Her temper flared as he opened the door of his
suite. All good intentions about apologising flew out of
the window. She was trapped! She tumbled to the
floor, watching him cross his arms and block her way
to the door. The outcome as far as Catherine was
concerned was frighteningly predictable.

'Conversation? I doubt you have much of that in
mind!' Kicking off her shoes, she tore like a tornado
into his bedroom. Flinging herself on the bed, she
regarded him scornfully. 'Wasn't this what you had
planned?' Her hand moved over the silken bedspread,
feeling it ripple sensuously beneath her fingers.

Steve followed her slowly, his eyes livid, brutal in

their impact. His shoulders were stiff, his mouth hard and tense.

'No, I want to make love to you, not tear you limb from limb.'

'Make love, Steve?' She ignored his warning, laughing painfully. 'What, as in "love them and leave them"? Very appropriate.'

'No,' he denied her accusation. 'As in love, live with her, marry her and give her children. I have no intention of leaving you tonight or for the foreseeable future. Now get off that damn bed and come and talk to me.'

Cat's dark eyes were hectic. She couldn't believe her ears. 'You don't have to tell me lies, Steve. You've told me quite clearly what you wanted from a relationship. I haven't forgotten.'

Steve came closer, his face stripped of pretence, his gaze blazing over her. 'And you told me you couldn't handle that!' he reminded her. 'I had no right to ask you. I'd taken too much already.'

Cat closed her eyes defeatedly. So that was it! She had thought him guilty of sharp practice, guilty of cold-hearted revenge, and now he was turning into a pillar of nobility in front of her eyes.

'You were my first lover——'

'Were!' He caught her to him, his hands biting into her upper arms, his teeth bared aggressively. 'What the hell do you mean by that?'

'Nothing. . .' She swallowed drily at the burning jealousy scarring his face. 'I just meant that you don't have to make promises because of that——'

Steve muttered something extremely insulting under his breath, one hand burying itself in the jet-black glory of her hair.

'I love you, you stupid woman! Look at me, for God's sake, I'm shaking with it.'

Cat's eyes widened in shock. She could feel the tremor in his body, see the defensive flicker of his lashes as he let his grip relax and regarded her defeatedly.

'I tried to pretend it wasn't happening. That you were just another pretty girl to pass the time with. I grew up with the idea that love was a weakness. . .a disease that left chaos in its wake. That was certainly my mother's experience and I swore I'd never repeat her mistake.' His eyes burnt into her, the message breathtakingly clear. 'I came back from the States to see you in danger of being thrown by Blood Star. That must have been the worst moment of my life. I thought I was going to lose you. . .' Closing his eyes in remembered pain, he shuddered. 'I've never felt so helpless in my life.'

Steve accepted her into his arms as she whispered his name in a plea, her face glowing as he finally convinced her of his sincerity. Cat's joy flamed in her eyes, her mouth tilted into a tremulous smile.

'You have very little faith in my ability on a horse,' she whispered.

'I'm savagely jealous of the time you spend with them,' he returned, his voice roughening.

Cat felt her love swell inside her until she felt she would burst. She had felt so vulnerable loving him; it was such a relief to find that he felt that way too.

'Stop towering above me.' She pouted up at him, her hands plucking at his T-shirt, wanting him to come down on to the bed and hold her close. Kneeling on the edge wasn't very comfortable.

'I get the feeling we won't do much talking if I come down there.'

Stripping off his T-shirt, he slid over her as she lay back against the luxurious surface. His gaze promised her a wicked number of sensual delights, his fingers brushing lightly from her neck to the tight curve of one thrusting breast, her breath laboured and shuddering in her throat when he squeezed gently, watching her eyes narrow in swift response.

'Is it the same for you, Catherine?' His hand moved to warm her belly, the flame material moving under his fingers, exaggerating the potency of his touch. The tide of silk rippled up over her thighs as he deliberately drew the material away from her flesh. 'Finding love here seemed impossible. I want to know. . .need to see how you feel.'

Cat was suddenly shy. 'I love you too,' she whispered, her eyes over-bright. 'When I thought you were just out for revenge, I. . .' She shook her head, unable to put the pain into words, but her face was stricken with memory. 'You must have known I loved you, when we made love. I didn't hide it very well.'

His mouth covered hers in a long passionate kiss. Cat's lips welcomed his, parting on a soft sigh, allowing him to plunder the soft inner flesh.

'I thought you loved me,' he muttered, some time later, against her throat, his mouth roaming restlessly against her skin. His hand ran up from her knee to the lacy suspenders and scrap of lace covering her loins. Heat ran under his skin as he viewed the dark arousal in her eyes. 'But then you'd gone when I got back to Ranleigh, and the next morning you were a twenty-four-carat bitch.'

'Steve,' she protested, humour briefly diluting the frenetic glitter between her lashes.

'My mother did a good job on you, didn't she? She told me what happened over the phone last night. She said if I couldn't tear myself away from the place, it must be love. I told her in no uncertain terms what I thought about her interfering. . .during which she hung up.' He viewed Cat with pained understanding. 'Her timing was perfect, wasn't it? I should have stayed with you. Selfish of me, but I needed those files so we wouldn't be interrupted in the morning.' His mouth formed a crooked smile. 'I wanted you thoroughly addicted before you left my bed.'

Cat was glad Sylvia Lucas had confessed. She hadn't liked the idea of causing trouble between mother and son. It also pleased her that business hadn't taken him from her that night.

'Now——' Steve traced the edge of one lacy suspender '—you know all my secrets.' Blue eyes sinfully drew her in. 'I want to acquaint myself with some of yours.'

Cat felt her heart shudder in her breast. Her mouth was consumed by his in a hungry storm of kisses. As a lover Steve was devastating. She wound herself around him sinuously as he brought her shiveringly alive, her clothes melting away under his touch, her inhibitions cast aside with them.

He pillaged her body, fully exploiting her potential to give him pleasure, but brought her gifts in return. She felt energised and exhausted by him until she twisted in a powerful climax of nerve-splintering ecstasy to lie spent against the tumble of bedding, her dark head thrown back, her breasts flushed as Steve bent over her, his throaty cry greeting his last powerful thrust into her body.

'Catherine.' He demanded that her eyes open and she let her lashes part, her tongue stroking her dry lips, her love naked for him to see, her satiation complete and gratifying.

'Thank you,' he offered with raw simplicity.

'Thank *you*,' she returned huskily, lifting her hand to stroke his jaw and feeling his lips seek her palm.

'We'll get married as soon as possible,' he stated possessively. 'I don't want to offend your mother but I want you living with me, not sneaking out of the cottage late at night.'

She was amused that he didn't consider a period of restraint but then, as always, Steve was being realistic.

'That's the second time you've mentioned marriage,' she chided him, 'and you haven't asked me yet.'

'Are you going to refuse?' His eyebrow lifted arrogantly.

'You're too sure of yourself, Mr Lucas.' She yelped as he tickled her and whispered, 'Yes,' delightedly to his demands for an answer to his proposal.

Her mirth subsided as she considered the nature of his job and the feelings he must have about living on the estate.

'Will we live at Ranleigh? Frank said you'd be moving on.'

'Our new business is mostly with Europe and Japan. Ranleigh is near enough Heathrow to be acceptable as a base.'

Cat's eyes darkened. 'I know, but——'

His mouth brushed over hers with erotic stealth, Cat's lips quivering with the friction. 'Bitterness can break you in two if you let it. Ranleigh is home because you're here. The past doesn't matter a damn compared with that.'

Cat wrapped her arms around his neck, kissing him deeply. 'I can't bear the thought of my father, and people I considered friends, treating you like that.'

'Don't think about it, then.' Steve's gaze bathed her in warmth. 'Think about something else instead.'

She smiled up at him, feeling his body stir against hers. 'We're supposed to be celebrating downstairs.'

'You're not going anywhere in that nightdress.' His smile touched her lips, her mind dazzled by the invitation in his gaze when he lifted his head, heated azure asking her to drown with him in the warm depths of love. 'Except bed, that is,' he added thickly.

'It is rather crumpled,' she agreed, her eyes seeking the puddle of red silk as he began a leisurely exploration of her throat. She closed her eyes in bliss at the shivers of pleasure he was creating, the apology she was supposed to make drifting into her mind.

'I'm sorry I thought so badly of you,' she murmured, her breath catching in her throat as his teeth nipped her. 'It must have seemed as if I was steeped in the Ranleigh tradition of snobbery and mistrust, just like the others.'

'I didn't give you much reason to trust me.' He lifted his head, his mouth curling in self-derision. 'Hotly pursuing a nineteen-year-old virgin isn't my style. It suited me to think you were trying to juice the company for every penny you could get,' he admitted, not looking very proud of himself. 'Otherwise, I would have felt a total bastard coming anywhere near you.' Dropping a swift kiss on her mouth, he regarded her with wry humour. 'I think we've both learnt things over the last few weeks that we needed badly.'

'Like my needing to give my castles in the air firm foundations?'

'Yes.' He searched her face, relieved that she accepted what he had tried to tell her all along. 'I tried to keep away to give you time to do it. I was scared you'd fall for the charms of some handsome young farmer.'

Cat smiled at the thought. She was a one-man

woman and was lucky enough to have her man equally besotted with her.

'Now, let's forget about the past and start a new, rather more interesting tradition. . .'

'What had you in mind?' Cat asked softly, her eyes eloquent as her fingers tangled in his hair.

But she knew already, before his very detailed explanation left her weak with desire. They would forge a new tradition at Ranleigh, washed clean of the vendettas of the past, one of joy and tenderness, a tradition of love.

MILLS & BOON

Always & Forever

This summer Mills & Boon presents the wedding
book of the year—three new full-length wedding
romances in one heartwarming volume.

Featuring top selling authors:

Debbie Macomber ♥ Jasmine Cresswell
Bethany Campbell

The perfect summer read!

Available: June 1995   Price: £4.99

MILLS & BOON

are proud to present...

A set of warm, involving romances in which you can meet
some fascinating members of our heroes' and heroines'
families. Published each month in the Romance series.

Look out for "A Family Closeness" by Emma Richmond
in June 1995.

Family Ties: Romances that take the family to heart.

FREE

Return this coupon and we'll send you 4 Mills & Boon romances and a mystery gift absolutely FREE! We'll even pay the postage and packing for you.

We're making you this offer to introduce you to the benefits of Reader Service: FREE home delivery of brand-new Mills & Boon romances, at least a month before they are available in the shops, FREE gifts and a monthly Newsletter packed with information.

Accepting these FREE books and gift places you under no obligation to buy, you may cancel at any time, even after receiving just your free shipment. Simply complete the coupon below and send it to:

HARLEQUIN MILLS & BOON, FREEPOST, PO BOX 70, CROYDON, CR9 9EL.

No stamp needed

Yes, please send me 4 free Mills & Boon romances and a mystery gift. I understand that unless you hear from me, I will receive 6 superb new titles every month for just £1.99* each postage and packing free. I am under no obligation to purchase any books and I may cancel or suspend my subscription at any time, but the free books and gifts will be mine to keep in any case. (I am over 18 years of age)

1EP5R

Ms/Mrs/Miss/Mr _____

Address _____

_____

_____ Postcode _____

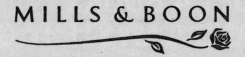

MILLS & BOON

Next Month's Romances

Each month you can choose from a wide variety of romance with Mills & Boon. Below are the new titles to look out for next month.

DEADLY RIVALS	Charlotte Lamb
TREACHEROUS LONGINGS	Anne Mather
THE TRUSTING GAME	Penny Jordan
WHEN ENEMIES MARRY...	Lindsay Armstrong
WANTED: WIFE AND MOTHER	Barbara McMahon
MASTER OF SEDUCTION	Sarah Holland
SAVAGE SEDUCTION	Sharon Kendrick
COME BACK FOREVER	Stephanie Howard
A FAMILY CLOSENESS	Emma Richmond
DANGEROUS NIGHTS	Rosalie Ash
HOUSE OF DREAMS	Leigh Michaels
DESERT MOON	Jennifer Taylor
PROGRESS OF PASSION	Alison Kelly
BITTERSWEET DECEPTION	Liz Fielding
UNTAMED MELODY	Quinn Wilder
RELUCTANT CHARADE	Margaret Callaghan